A Second Coming by Richard Marsh

Richard Bernard Heldmann was born on 12th October 1857, in St Johns Wood, North London.

By his early 20's Heldmann began publishing fiction for the myriad magazine publications that had sprung up and were eager for good well-written content.

In October 1882, Heldmann was promoted to co-editor of Union Jack, a popular magazine, but his association with the publication ended suddenly in June 1883. It appears Heldman was prone to issuing forged cheques to finance his lifestyle. In April 1884 He was sentenced to 18 months hard labour.

In order to be well away from the scandal and damage this had caused to his reputation Heldmann adopted a pseudonym on his release from jail. Shortly thereafter the name 'Richard Marsh' began to appear in the literary periodicals. The use of his mother's maiden name as part of it seems both a release and a lifeline.

A stroke of very good fortune arrived with his novel The Beetle published in 1897. This would turn out to be his greatest commercial success and added some much-needed gravitas to his literary reputation.

Marsh was a prolific writer and wrote almost 80 volumes of fiction as well as many short stories, across many genres from horror and crime to romance and humour.

Index of Contents

'If,' asked the Man in the Street, 'Christ were to come again to London, in this present year of grace, how would He be received, and what would happen?'

'I will try to show you,' replied the Scribe.

These following pages represent the Scribe's attempt to achieve the impossible.

PART I

THE TALES WHICH WERE TOLD

Chapter I

The Interrupted Dinner

He stood at the corner of the table with his hat and overcoat on, just as he had rushed into the room.

'Christ has come again!'

The servants were serving the entrees. Their breeding failed them. They stopped to stare at Chisholm. The guests stared too, those at the end leaning over the board to see him better. He looked like a man newly startled out of dreaming, blinking at the lights and glittering table array. His hat was a little on one side of his head. He was hot and short of breath, as if he had been running. They regarded him as a little bewildered, while he, on his part, looked back at them as if they were the creatures of a dream.

'Christ has come again!'

He repeated the words in a curious, tremulous, sobbing voice, which was wholly unlike his own.

Conversation had languished. Just before his entrance there had been one of those prolonged pauses which, to an ambitious hostess, are as a sound of doom. The dinner bade fair to be a failure. If people will not talk, to offer them to eat is vain. Criticism takes the place of appetite. Amplett looked, for him, bad-tempered. He was leaning back in his chair, smiling wryly at the wineglass which he was twiddling between his fingers. His wife, on the contrary, sat very upright—with her an ominous sign. She looked straight in front of her, with a tender softness in her glance which only to those who did not know her suggested paradise. Over the whole table there was an air of vague depression, an irresistible tendency to be bored.

Chisholm's unceremonious entry created a diversion. It filliped the atmosphere. Amplett's bad temper vanished on the instant.

'Hollo, Hugh! thought you weren't coming. Sit down, man; in your coat and hat if you like, only do sit down!'

Chisholm eyed him as if not quite certain that it was he who was being spoken to, or who the speaker was. There was that about his bearing which seemed to have a singular effect upon his host. Amplett, leaning farther over the table, called to him in short, sharp tones:

'Why do you stand and look like that? What's the matter?'

'Christ has come again!'

As he repeated the words for the third time, there was in his voice a note of exultation which was in odd dissonance with what was generally believed to be his character. The self-possession for which he was renowned seemed to have wholly deserted him. Something seemed to have shaken his nature to its depths; he who was used to declare that life could offer nothing which was of interest to him.

People glanced at each other, and at the strange-looking man at the end of the table. Was he mad or drunk? As if in answer to their glances he stretched out his hands a little in front of him, saying:

'It is true! It is true! Christ has come again! I have come from His presence here to you!'

Mrs. Amplett's voice rang out sharply:

'Hugh, what is the matter with you? Are you insane?'

'I was insane. Now I am wise. I know, for I have seen. I have been among the first to see.'

There was something in his manner which affected them strangely. A wildness, an exultation, an intensity! If it had not been so entirely out of keeping with the man's everyday disposition it might not have seemed so curious. But those who knew him best were moved most. They were aware that his nerves were not easily affected; that something extraordinary must have occurred to have produced this bearing. Clement Fordham rose from his chair and went to him.

'Come, Hugh, tell me what's wrong outside.'

He made as if to slip his arm through Chisholm's, who would have none of it. He held Fordham off with hand extended.

'Thank you, Fordham, but for the present I'll stay here. I am not mad, nor have I been drinking. I'm as sober and as sane as you.'

A voice came down the table, Bertie Vaughan's. In it there was a ring of laughter:

'Tell us, Chisholm, what you've seen.'

'I will tell you.'

Chisholm removed his hat, as if suddenly remembering that he had it on. He rested the brim against the edge of the table, looking down the two rows of faces towards Amplett at the end. Mrs. Amplett interposed:

'Hadn't you better sit down, Hugh, and have something to eat? The entrees are getting cold. Or you might tell your story after we've finished dinner. Hunger magnifies; wonders grow less when one has dined.'

There was a chorus of dissentient voices.

'No, no, Mrs. Amplett. Let him tell his story now.'

'I will tell it to you now.'

The hostess gave way. Chisholm told his tale. He riveted his auditors' attention. The servants listened openly.

'I walked here. As you know, the night is fine, and I thought the stroll would do me good. As I was passing through Bryanston Square a man came round the corner on a bicycle. The road has recently been watered, and is still wet and greasy. His tyre must have skidded, or something, because he entirely lost control of his machine, and went dashing into the hydrant which stands by the kerb. He was moving pretty fast, and as it came into contact with the hydrant his machine was splintered, and he was pitched over the handle-bar heavily on to his head. He was some fifteen or twenty yards from where I was. I went to him as rapidly as I could, but by the time I reached him he was already dead.'

'Dead!'

The word came in a sort of chorus from half a dozen throats.

'Dead,' repeated Chisholm.

'Are you sure that he was dead?'

The question came from Amplett.

'Certain. He was a very unpleasant sight. He must have fallen with more violence even than I had supposed. His skull was shattered. He must have come down on it on the hard road, and then twisted over on to his back. He was a big, heavy man, and the wrench which he had given himself in rolling over had broken his neck. I was so astonished to find him dead, and at the spectacle which he presented, that for a second or two I was at a loss as to what steps I ought to take. No other person was in the square, and, so far as I could judge, the accident had not been witnessed from either of the windows. While I hesitated, on a sudden I was conscious that someone was at my side.'

He stopped as if to take breath. There came a rain of questions.

'Someone? What do you mean by someone?'

'I will try and tell you exactly what I saw. It is not easy. I am yet too near—fresh from the Presence.'

He clasped his hands a little more tightly on the brim of his hat, then closed his eyes for a second or two, opening them to look straight down the table, as if endeavouring to bring well within the focus of his vision something which was there.

'I was looking down at the dead man as he lay there in an ugly heap, conscious that I was due for dinner, and wondering what steps I ought to take. I felt no interest in him—none whatever; neither his living nor his dying was anything to me. My chief feeling was one of annoyance that he should have chosen that moment to fall dead right in my path; it was an unwarrantable intrusion of his affairs into mine. As I stood, I knew that someone was on his other side, looking down at him with me. And I was afraid—yes, I was afraid.'

The speaker had turned pale—the pallor of fear had come upon the cheeks of the man whose imperturbable courage had been proved a hundred times. His voice sank lower.

'For some moments I continued with eyes cast down; I did not dare to look up. At last, when my pulse grew a little calmer, I ventured to raise my eyes. On the other side of the dead bicyclist was one who was in the figure of a man. I knew that it was Christ.'

He spoke with an accent of intense conviction, the like of which his hearers had never heard from the lips of anyone before. It was as though Chisholm spoke with the faith which can move mountains. Those who listened were perforce dumb.

'His glance met mine. I knew myself to be the thing I was. I was ashamed. He pointed to the body lying in the roadway, saying: "Your brother sleeps?" I could not answer. Seeing that I was silent, He spoke again: "Are you not of one spirit and of one flesh? I come to wake your brother out of slumber." He inclined His hand towards the dead man, saying: "Arise, you who sleep." Immediately he that was dead stood up. He seemed bewildered, and exclaimed as in a fit of passion: "That's a nice spill. Curse the infernal slippery road!" Then he turned and saw Who was standing at his side. As he did so, he burst into a storm of tears, crying like a child; and when he cried, He that had been there was not. The bicyclist and I were alone together.'

A pause followed Chisholm's words.

'And then what happened?'

The query came from Mrs. Amplett.

'Nothing happened. I hurried off as fast as I could, for I was still afraid, and left the bicyclist sobbing in the roadway.'

There was another interval of silence, until Gregory Hawkes, putting his eyeglass in its place, fixedly regarded Chisholm.

'Are we to accept this as a sober narrative of actual fact, or—where's the joke?'

'I have told you the truth. Christ has come again!'

'Christ in Bryanston Square!'

Mr. Hawkes's tone was satirical.

'Yes, Christ in Bryanston Square. Why not in Bryanston Square if on the hill of Calvary? Is not this His own city?'

'His own city!'

Again there was the satiric touch.

One of the servants, dropping a dish, began to excuse himself.

'Pardon me, sir, but I'm a Seventh–Day Christian, and I've been looking for the Second Coming these three years now, and more. Hearing from Mr. Chisholm that it's come at last has made me feel a little nervous.'

Mrs. Amplett turned to the butler.

'Goss, let the servants leave the room.'

They went, as if they bore their tails between their legs, some with the entrée dishes still in their hands.

'I wish,' murmured Bertie Vaughan,' that this little incident could have been conveniently postponed till after we had dined.'

Arthur Warton, of St. Ethelburga's, showed signs of disapprobation.

'I believe that I am as broad-minded a priest as you will easily find, but there are seasons at which certain topics should not be touched upon. Without wishing in any way to thrust forward my clerical office, I would point out to Mr. Chisholm that this assuredly is one.'

'Is there then a season at which Christ should not come again?'

'Mr. Chisholm!'

'Or in which He should not restore the dead to life?'

'I should not wish to disturb the harmony of the gathering, Mr. Amplett, but I am afraid the—eh— circumstances are not—eh—fortuitous. I cannot sit here and allow my sacred office to be mocked.'

'Mocked! Is it to mock your sacred office to spread abroad the news that He has come again? I am fresh from His presence, and tell you so—you that claim to be His priest.'

Fordham, who had been standing by him all the time, came a little closer.

'Come, Hugh, let's get out of this, you and I, and talk over things quietly together.'

Again Chisholm kept him from him with his outstretched hand.

'In your tone, Fordham, more even than in your words, there is suggestion. Of what? that I am mad? You have known me all my life. Have I struck you as being of the stuff which makes for madness? As a victim of hysteria? As a subject of hallucinations? As a liar? I am as sane as you, as clear-headed, as matter-of-fact, as truthful. I tell you, in very truth and very deed, that to-night I have seen Christ hard by here in the square.'

'My dear fellow, these people have come here to dine.'

'Is, then, dinner more than Christ?'

Smiling his easy, tolerant smile, Fordham touched Chisholm lightly with his fingers on the arm.

'My very dear old chap, this sort of thing is so awfully unlike you, don't you know?'

'You, also, will be changed when you have seen Christ. Fordham, I have seen Christ!'

The intensity of his utterance seemed to strike his hearers a blow. The women shivered, turning pale—even those who were painted. Mr. Warton leaned across the table towards Mrs. Amplett.

'I really think that you ladies had better retire. Our friend seems to be in a curious mood.'

The hostess nodded. She rose from her seat, looking very queerly at Mr. Chisholm, for whom her penchant is well known. The other women followed her example. The rustling concourse fluttered from the room, the Incumbent of St. Ethelburga holding the door open to let them pass, and himself bringing up the rear. The laymen were left alone together, Chisholm and Fordham standing at the head of the table with, on their faces, such very different expressions.

The host seemed snappish.

'You see what you've done? I offer you my congratulations, Mr. Chisholm. I don't know if you call the sort of thing with which you have been favouring us good form.'

'Is good form more than Christ?'

Amplett made an impatient sound with his lips. He stood up.

'Upon my word of honour, Mr. Chisholm, you must be either drunk or mad. I trust, for your own sake, that you are merely mad. Come, gentlemen, let's join the ladies.'

The men quitted the room in a body. Only Clement Fordham stayed with his friend. Chisholm watched them as they went. Then, when the last had gone and the door was closed, he turned to his companion.

'Yet it is the truth that this night I have seen Christ!'

The other laughed.

'Then, in that case, let's hope that you won't see much more of Him—no impiety intended, I assure you. Now let you and me take our two selves away.'

He slipped his arm through his friend's. As they were about to move, the door opened and a servant entered. It was the man who had dropped the dish. He approached Chisholm with stuttering tongue.

'Pardon me, sir, if I seem to take a liberty, but might I ask if the Second Coming has really come at last? As a Seventh–Day Christian it's a subject in which I take an interest, and the fact is that there's a difference of opinion between my wife and me as to whether it's to be this year or next.'

The man bore ignorance on his countenance written large, and worse. Hugh Chisholm turned from him with repugnance.

'He's your brother,' whispered Fordham in his ear, as they moved towards the door.

The expression of Hugh Chisholm's face was stern.

Chapter II

The Woman and the Coats

Mr. Davis looked about him with bloodshot eyes. His battered bowler was perched rakishly on the back of his head, and his hands were thrust deep into his trousers pockets. He did not seem to find the aspect of the room enlivening. His wife, standing at a small oblong deal table, was making a parcel of two black coats to which she had just been giving the finishing stitches. The man, the woman, the table, and the coats, practically represented the entire contents of the apartment.

The fact appeared to cause Mr. Davis no slight dissatisfaction. His bearing, his looks, his voice, all betrayed it.

'I want some money,' he observed.

'Then you'll have to want,' returned his wife.

'Ain't you got none?'

'No, nor shan't have, not till I've took these two coats in.'

'Then what'll it be?'

'You know very well what it'll be—three-and-six—one-and-nine apiece—if there ain't no fines.'

'And this is what they call the land of liberty, the 'ome of the free, where people slave and slave—for one-and-nine.'

Mr. Davis seemed conscious that the conclusion of his sentence was slightly impotent, and spat on the floor as if to signify his regret.

"Tain't much slaving you do, anyhow.'

'No, nor it ain't much I'm likely to do; I'm no servile wretch; I'm free-born.'

'Prefers to make your living off me, you do.'

'Well, and why not? Ain't woman the inferior animal? Didn't Nature mean it to be her pride to minister to man? Ain't it only the false veneer of a rotten civilization what's upset all that? If I gives my talents for the good of the species, as I do do, as is well known I do do, ain't it only right that you should give me something in return, if it's only a crust and water? Ain't that law and justice—natural law, mind you, and natural justice?'

'I don't know nothing about law, natural or otherwise, but I do know it ain't justice.'

Mr. Davis looked at his wife, more in sorrow than in anger. He was silent for some seconds, as if meditating on the peculiar baseness of human nature. When he spoke there was a whine in his raucous voice, which was, perhaps, meant to denote his consciousness of how much he stood in need of sympathy.

'I'm sorry, Matilda, to hear you talk to me like that, because it forces me to do something what I shouldn't otherwise have done. Give me them coats.'

She had just finished packing up the coats in the linen wrapper, and was pinning up one end. Snatching up the parcel, she clasped it to her bosom as if it had been some precious thing.

'No, Tommy, not the coats!'

'Matilda, once more I ask you to give me them coats.'

'What do you want them for?'

'Once more, Matilda, I ask you to give me them coats.'

'No, Tommy, that I won't—never! not if you was to kill me! You know what happened the last time, and all I had to go through; and you promised you'd never do it again, and you shan't, not while I can help it—no, that you shan't!'

Clasping the parcel tightly to her, she drew back towards a corner of the room, like some wild creature standing at bay. Mr. Davis, advancing towards the table, leaned on it, addressing her as if he desired to impress her with the fact that he was endeavouring not to allow his feelings to get the better of his judgment.

'Listen to me, Matilda. I'm soft and tender, as well you know, and should therefore regret having to start knocking you about; but want is want, and I want 'arf a sovereign this day, and have it I must.'

'What do you want it for?'

Mr. Davis brought his clenched fist sharply down upon the table—possibly by way of a hint.

'Never you mind what I want it for. I do want it, and that's enough for you. You trouble yourself with your own affairs, and don't poke your nose into mine, my girl; you'll find it safest.'

'I'll try to get it for you, Tommy.'

Mr. Davis was scornful.

'Oh, you will, will you! How are you going to set about getting 'arf a sovereign? Perhaps you'll be so good as to let me know. Because if you can lay hands on 'arf a sovereign whenever one's wanted, it's a trick worth knowing. You're such a clever one at getting 'old of the pieces, you are, and always have been.'

The man's irony seemed to cause the woman to wince. She drew a little farther back towards her corner.

'I don't rightly know how I shall get hold of it, not just now, I don't; but I daresay I shall manage somehow.'

'Oh, you do, do you? Shall I tell you how you'll manage? You listen to me. You'll go to them there slave-drivers with them two coats, and they'll keep you waiting for two mortal hours or more. Then they'll dock sixpence for fines—you're always getting fined; you 'ardly ever take anything in without you're fined; you're a slovenly workwoman, that's what you are, my lass, and that's the truth!—you'll come away with three bob, and spend 'arf a crown on rent, or some such silly nonsense; and then when it comes to me, you'll start snivelling, and act the crybaby, and I shall have to treat you to a kicking, and find myself further off my 'arf sovereign than ever I was. I don't want no more of your nonsense. Give me them two coats!'

'You'll pawn 'em if I do.'

'Of course I'll pawn 'em. What do you suppose I'm going to do with them—eat 'em, or give them to the Queen?'

'You'll get me into trouble again! They're due in today. You know what happened last time. If they lock me up again, I'll be sent away.'

'Then be sent away, and be 'anged to you for a nasty, mean, snivelling cat! Why don't you earn enough to keep your 'usband like a gentleman? If you don't, it's your fault, isn't it? Give me them two coats!'

'No, Tommy, I won't!'

He went closer to her.

'For the last time; will you give me them two coats?'

'No!'

She hugged the parcel closer, and she closed her eyes, so that she should not see him strike her. He hit her once, twice, thrice, choosing his mark with care and discretion. Under the first two blows she reeled; the last sent her in a heap to the floor. When she was down he kicked her in a business-like, methodical fashion, then picked up the parcel which had fallen from her grasp.

'You've brought it on yourself, as you very well know. It's the kind of thing I don't care to have to do. I'm not like some, what's always spoiling to knock their wives about; but when I do have to do it, there's no one does it more thorough, I will say that.'

He left her lying in a heap on the boards. On his way to the pawnbroker's he encountered a friend, Joe Cooke. Mr. Cooke stopped and hailed him.

'What yer, Tommy! Are you coming along with us to-night on that there little razzle?'

'Of course I am. Didn't I say I was? And when I say I'm coming, don't I always come?'

'All right, old coxybird! Keep your 'air on! No one said you didn't. Got the rhino?'

'I have. Leastways, I soon shall have, when I've turned this little lot into coin of the realm.'

He pointed to the bundle which he bore beneath his arm. Mr. Cooke grinned.

'What yer got there?'

'I've got a couple of coats what my wife's been wearing out her eyes on for a set of slave-driving sweaters. Three-and-six they was to pay her for them. I rather reckon that I'll get more than three-and-six for them, unless I'm wrong. And when I have melted 'em, Joe, I don't mind if I do you a wet.'

Joe did not mind, either. The two fell in side by side. Mr. Cooke drew his hand across his mouth.

'Ever since my old woman died I've felt I ought to have another—a good one, mind you. There's nothing like having someone to whom you can turn for a bob or so.'

'It's more than a bob or so I get out of my old woman, you may take my word. If she don't keep me like a gentleman, she hears of it.'

Mr. Cooke regarded his friend with genuine admiration.

'Ah! but we're not all so fly as you, Tommy, nor yet so lucky.'

'Perhaps not—not, mind you, that that's owing to any fault of yours. It's as we're made.'

Mr. Davis, with the bundle under his arm, bore himself with an air of modest pride, as one who appreciated his natural advantages.

They reached the pawnbroker's. The entrance to the pledge department was in a little alley leading off the main street. As Mr. Davis stood at the mouth of this alley to say a parting word to his friend as a prelude to the important business of the pledging, someone touched him on the arm.

A voice accosted him.

'What is it that you would do?'

Mr. Davis spun round like a teetotum. He stared at the Stranger.

'Hollo, matey! Who are you?'

'I am He that you know not of.'

Mr. Davis drew a little back, as if a trifle disconcerted. His voice was huskier than even it was wont to be.

'What's the little game?'

'I bid you tell me what is this thing that you would do?'

Mr. Davis seemed to find in the words, which were quietly uttered, a compelling influence which made him curiously frank.

'I am going to pawn these here two coats which my wife's been making.'

'Is it well?'

Mr. Davis slunk farther from the Stranger. 'What's it got to do with you?'

'Is it well?'

There was a sorrowful intonation in the repetition of the inquiry, blended with a singularly penetrant sternness. Mr. Davis cowered as if he had been struck a blow. He turned to his friend.

'Say, Joe, who is this bloke?'

The Stranger spoke to Mr. Cooke.

'Look on Me, and you shall know.'

Mr. Cooke looked—and knew. He began to tremble as if he would have fallen to the ground. Mr. Davis, noting his friend's condition, became uneasy.

'Say, Joe, what's the matter with you? What's he done to you, Joe?'

Mr. Cooke was silent. The Stranger answered:

'Would that that which has been done to him could be done to you, and to all this city! But you are of those that cannot know, for in them is no knowledge. Yet return to your wife, and make your peace with her, lest worse befall.'

Mr. Davis began to slink out of the alley, with furtive air and face carefully averted from the Stranger. As he reached the pavement, a big man, with a scarlet handkerchief twisted round his neck, caught him by the shoulder. The big man's speech was flavoured with adjectives.

'Why, Tommy! what's up with you? You look as if you was just a-going to see Jack Ketch.'

Then came the flood of adjectives to give the sentence balance. Mr. Davis tried to wriggle from his questioner's too strenuous grip.

'Let me go, Pug—let me go!'

'What for? What's wrong? Who's been doing something to yer?'

Mr. Davis made a movement of his head towards the Stranger. He spoke in a husky whisper.

'That bloke—over there.'

The big man dragged the unwilling Mr. Davis forward.

'What's my friend been doing to you, and what have you been doing to him?'

There was the usual adjectival torrent. The Stranger replied to the inquiry with another.

'Why are you so unclean of mouth? Is it because you are unclean of heart, or because you do not know what the things are which you utter?'

The retorted question seemed to take the big man aback. His manner became still more blusterous:

'I don't want none of your lip, and I won't have any, and you can take that from me! I don't know what kind of a Gospel-pitcher you are; but if you think because preaching's your lay that you can come it over me, I'll just show you can't by knocking the head right off yer.'

'What big things the little say!'

The retort seemed to goad Mr. Davis's friend to a state of considerable excitement.

'Little, am I? I'll show you! I'll learn you! I'll give you a lesson free gratis, and for nothing now, right straight off.' He began to tear off his cap and coat. 'Here, some of you chaps, catch hold while I'm a-showing him!' As he turned up his shirtsleeves, he addressed the crowd which had gathered: 'These blokes come to us, and because we're poor they think they can treat us as if we was dirt, and come the pa and ma game over us as if we was a lot of kids. I've had enough of it—in fact, I've had too much. For the future I mean to set about every one of them as tries to come it over me. Now, then, my bloke, put up your dooks or eat your words. Don't think you're going to get out of it by standing still, because if you don't beg pardon for what you said to me just now I'll—'

The man, who was by profession a pugilist, advanced towards the Stranger in professional style. The Stranger raised His right hand.

'Stay! and let your arm be withered. Better lose your arm than all that you have.'

Before the eyes of those who were standing by the man's arm began to dwindle till there was nothing protruding from the shirtsleeve which he had rolled up to his shoulder but a withered stump. The man stood as if rooted to the ground, the expression of his countenance so changed as to amount to complete transfiguration. The crowd was still until a voice inquired of the Stranger:

'Who are you?'

The Stranger pointed to the man whose arm was withered.

'Can you not see? The world still looks for a sign.'

There were murmurs among the people.

'He's a conjurer!'

'The bloke's a mesmerist, that's what he is!'

'He's one of those hanky-panky coves!'

'I am none of these things. I come from a city not built of hands to this city of man's glory and his shame to bring to you a message—no new thing, but that old one which the world has forgotten.'

'What's the message, Guv'nor?'

'Those who see Me and know Me will know what is My message; those who know Me not, neither will they know My message.'

Mr. Cooke fell on his knees on the pavement.

'Oh, Guv'nor, what shall I do?'

'Cease to weep; there are more than enough tears already.'

'I'm only a silly fool, Guv'nor; tell me what I ought to do.'

'Do well; be clean; judge no one.'

A woman came hurrying through the crowd. It was Mrs. Davis. At sight of her husband she burst into exclamations:

'Oh, Tommy, have you pawned them?'

'No, Matilda, I haven't, and I'm not going to, neither.'

'Thank God!'

She threw her arms about her husband's neck and kissed him.

'That is good hearing,' said the Stranger.

The people's attention had been diverted by Mrs. Davis's appearance. When they turned again to look for the Stranger He was gone.

Chapter III

The Words of the Preacher

'They say that the Jews do not look forward to the rebuilding of their Holy City of Jerusalem, to their return to the Promised Land. They say that we Christians do not look forward to the Second Coming of Christ. As to the indictment against the Chosen People, we will not pronounce: we are not Jews. But as to the charge against us Christians, there we are on firmer ground. We can speak, and we must. My answer is, It's a lie. We do look forward to His Second Coming. We watch and wait for it. It is the subject of our constant prayers. We have His promise, in words which cannot fail. The whole fabric of our faith is built upon our assurance of His return. If the delay seems long, it is because, in His sight, a thousand years are as a day. Who are we to time His movements, and fix the hour of His coming so that it may fall in with our convenience? We know that He will come, in His own time, in His own way. He will forgive us if we strain our eyes eastward, watching for the first rays of the dawn to gild the mountains and the plains, and herald the glory of His advent. But beyond that His will, not ours, be done. We know, O Lord Christ, Thou wilt return when it seems well in Thy sight.'

The Rev. Philip Evans was a short, somewhat sturdily built man, who was a little too heavy for his height. His dress was, to all intents and purposes, that of a layman, though something about the colour and cut of the several garments suggested the dissenting minister of a certain modern type. He was a hairy man; his brown hair, beard, and whiskers were just beginning to be touched with gray. He wore spectacles, big round glasses, set in bright steel frames. He had a trick of snatching at them with his left hand every now and then, as if to twitch them straight upon his nose. He was not an orator, but was something of a rhetorician. He had the gift of the gab, and the present-day knack of treating what are supposed to be sacred subjects in secular fashion—of 'bringing them down,' as he himself described it, 'to the intelligence' of his hearers, apparently unconscious of the truth that what he supposed to be their standard of intelligence was, in fact, his own.

There was about his manner, methods, gestures, voice, a species of nervous force, the product of restlessness rather than vitality, which attracted the sort of persons to whom he specially appealed, when they had nothing better to do, and held them, if not so firmly as the music-hall and theatrical performances which they preferentially patronised, still, with a sufficient share of interest. The band and the choir had something to do with the success which attended his labours. But, after all, these were merely side-shows. Indubitably the chief attraction was the man himself, and the air of brightness and 'go' which his personality lent to the proceedings. One never knew what would be the next thing he would say or do.

That Sunday evening the great hall was thronged. It nearly always was. In the great thoroughfare without the people passed continually to and fro, a motley crowd, mostly in pursuit of mischief. All sorts and conditions of persons, as they neared the entrance, would come in, if only to rest for a few minutes, and listen by the way, and look on. There was a constant coming and going. Philip Evans was one of the sights of town, not the least of its notorieties; and those very individuals against whom his diatribes were principally directed found, upon occasion, a moderate degree of entertainment in listening to examples of his comminatory thunders.

The subject of his evening's discourse had been announced as 'The Second Coming: Is it Fact or Dream?' He had chosen as his text the eleventh verse of the third chapter of St. John's Revelation: 'Behold, I come quickly; hold fast that which thou hast, that no man take thy crown.' He had pointed out to his audience that these words were full of suggestion, even apart from their context; preeminently so in connection with it. They had in them, he maintained, Christ's own promise that He would return to the world in which He had endured so much disappointment and suffering, such ignominy and such shame. He supported his assertion by the usual cross references to Biblical passages, construing them to suit his arguments by the dogmatic methods with which custom has made us familiar.

'If there is one thing sure, it is the word of Jesus Christ; if there is one thing Christ has promised us, it is that He will return. If we believe that He came once, we must believe that He will come again. We have no option, unless we make out Christ to be a liar. There was no meaning in his First Coming unless it is His intention to return. The work He began has to be finished. If you deny a personal Christ, then you are at least logical in regarding His whole story as allegorical, the story that He was and will be; in which case may He help you, and open your eyes that you may see. But if you are a Christian, it is because you believe in Christ, the living Christ, the very Christ, the Christ made man, that was and will be. Your faith, our faith, is not a symbol, it's a fact. It's a solid thing, not the distillation of a dream. We believe that Jesus Christ was like unto us, hungry as we are, and athirst; that He felt as we feel, knew our joys and sorrows, our trials and temptations. He came to us once, that is certain. To attempt to whittle away that fact is to make of our Christianity a laughing-stock, and our plight most lamentable. Better for us, a thousand, thousand times, that we had never been born! But He came—we know He came! And, knowing that, we know that we have His promise that He will come again, and rejoice!

'Of the time and manner of His Second Coming there is none mortal that may certainly speak. To pretend to speak on the subject with special insight or knowledge would be intolerable presumption—worse, akin to blasphemy! Thy will, not ours, be done. We only stand and wait. In Thy hand, Lord God, is the issue. We know it, and give thanks. But while recognising our inability to probe into the workings of the Most High, I think we may be excused if we make certain reflections on the theme which to us, as Christians, is of such vital moment.

'First, as to the time. Knowing nothing, we do know this, that it may be at any instant of any hour of any day. The Lord Jesus Christ may be speeding to us now. He may be in our midst even while I speak. Why not? We know that He was in a certain synagogue while service was taking place, without any there having had the slightest warning of His intended presence. What He did then can He not do now? And will He not? Who shall say?

'For, as to the manner, we can at least venture to say this, that we know not, with any sort of certainty, what the manner of His coming will be. The dark passages of the Scripture are dark perhaps of intention, and, maybe, will continue obscure, until in the fulness of time all things are made plain. There are those who affirm that He will come with pomp and power, in the fulness of His power, as a conquering king, with legions of angels, to be the Judge of all the earth. To me it appears that those who say this go further than the evidence before us warrants. And it may be observed that precisely the same views were held by a large section of the Jews in the year of our Lord. They thought that He would come in the splendour of His majesty. And because He did not, they hung Him on the tree. Let us not stand in peril of the same mistake. As He came before, in the simple garb of a simple man, may He not come in that same form again? Why not? Who are we that we should answer? I adjure you, in His most holy Name, to keep on this matter an open mind, lest we be guilty of the same sin as those purblind Jews.

'What we have to do is to know Him when He does come. The notion that we shall be sure to do so seems to me to be born of delusion. Did the Jews know Him when He came before? No! Why? Because He was a contradiction of all their preconceived ideas. They expected one thing, and found another. They looked for a king in his glittering robes; and, instead, there was a Man who had not where to lay His head. There is the crux of the matter; because He was so like themselves, they did not know Him for what He was. The difference was spiritual, whereas they expected it to be material. The tendency of the world is now, as it was then, to look at the material side. Let us be careful that we are not deceived. It is by the spirit we shall know Him when He comes!'

The words had been rapidly spoken, and the preacher paused at this point, perhaps to take breath, or perhaps to collect his thoughts prior to diverting the current of his discourse into a slightly different channel. At any rate, there was a distinct pause in the flow of language. While it continued, Someone stood up in the body of the hall, and a Voice inquired:

'Who shall know Him when He comes?'

The question was clearly audible all over the building. It was by no means unusual, in that place, for incidents to occur which were not in accordance with the programme. Interruptions were not infrequent. Both preacher and people were used to them. By a considerable part of the audience such interludes were regarded as not the least interesting portion of the proceedings. To the fashion in which he was wont to deal with such incidents the Rev. Philip Evans owed, in no slight degree, his vogue. It was his habit to lose neither his presence of mind nor his temper. He was, after his manner, a fighter born. Seldom did he show to more advantage than in dealing out cut-and-thrust to a rash intervener.

When the Voice asking the question rose from the body of the hall, there were those who at once concluded that such an intervention had occurred. For the instant, the movement in and out of the doors ceased. Heads were craned forward, and eyes and ears strained to lose nothing of what was about to happen. Mr. Evans, to whom the question seemed addressed, appeared to be no whit taken by surprise. His retort was prompt:

'Sir, pray God that you may know Him when He comes.'

The Voice replied:

'I shall know as I shall be known. But who is there shall know Me?'

The Speaker moved towards the platform, threading His way between the crowded rows of seats with an ease and a celerity which seemed strange. None endeavoured to stop Him. Philip Evans remained silent and motionless, watching Him as He came.

When the Stranger had gained the platform, He turned towards the people, asking:

'Who is there here that knows Me? Is there one?' There was not one that answered. He turned to the preacher. 'Look at Me well. Do you not know Me?'

For once in a way Philip Evans seemed uncomfortable and ill at ease and abashed.

'How shall I know you, since you are to me a stranger?'

'And yet you have looked for My coming?'

'Your coming? Who are you?'

'Look at Me well. Is there nothing by which you may know Me?'

'I may have seen you before; but, if so, I have certainly forgotten it, which is the more strange, since your face is an unusual one.'

'Oh, you Christians, that preach of what you have no knowledge, and lay down the law of which you have no understanding!' He turned to the people. 'You followers of Christ, that never knew Him, and never shall, and would not if you could, yet make a boast of His name, and blazon it upon your foreheads, crying, Behold His children! You call upon Him in the morning and at night, careless if He listen, and fearful lest He hear; saying, with your lips, "We look for His coming"; and, with your hearts, "Send it not in our time." It is by the spirit you shall know Him. Yes, of a truth. Is there not one among you in whom the spirit is? Is there not one?'

The Stranger stood with His arms extended in front of Him, in an attitude of appeal. The hush of a perfect silence reigned in the great hall. Every countenance was turned to Him, but so far as could be seen, not a muscle moved. The predominant expression upon the expanse of faces was astonishment, mingled with curiosity. His arms sank to His sides.

'He came unto His own, and His own knew Him not!'

The words fell from His lips in tones of infinite pathos. He passed from the platform through the hall, and out of the door, followed by the eyes of all who were there, none seeking to stay Him.

When He had gone, one of the persons who were associated with the conduct of the service went up to Mr. Evans. A few whispered words were exchanged between them. Then this person, going to the edge of the platform, announced:

'After what has just occurred, I regret to have to inform you that Mr. Evans feels himself unable to continue his address. He trusts to be able, God willing, to bring it to a close on a more auspicious occasion. This evening's service will be brought to a conclusion by singing the hymn "Lo, He comes, in clouds descending!"'

Chapter IV

The Children's Mother

'You've had your pennyworth.'

'Oh, Charlie, I haven't! you must send me higher. You mustn't stop; I've only just begun to swing.'

'I shall stop; it's my turn. You'd keep on for ever.'

The boy drew to one side. The swing began to slow. Doris grew indignant. She endeavoured to swing herself, wriggling on the seat, twisting herself in various attitudes. The result was failure. The swing moved slower. She tried a final appeal.

'Oh, Charlie, I do think you might push me just a little longer; it's not fair. You said you'd give me a good one. Then I'll give you a splendid swing.'

'You've had a good one. You'd keep on for ever, you would. Get off!'

The swing stopped dead. The girl made a vain attempt to give it momentum.

'It's beastly of you,' she said.

She scrambled to the ground. The boy got on. He was not content to sit; he stood upright.

'Now, then,' he cried, 'why don't you start me? Don't you see I'm ready?'

'You'll tumble off. Mamma said you weren't to stand.'

'Shall stand. Go and tell! Start me!'

'You will tumble.'

'All right, then, I will tumble. Start me! Don't you hear?'

She 'started' him. The swing having received its initial impetus, he swung himself. He mounted higher and higher. Doris watched him, leaning her right shoulder against the beech tree, her hands behind her back. She interpolated occasional remarks on the risk which he was running.

'You'll fall if you don't take care. You oughtn't to go so high. Mamma said you oughtn't to go so high.'

He received her observations with scorn.

'Just as though I will fall! How silly you are! You will keep on!'

As he spoke, one of the ropes gave way. The other rope swerving, he was dashed against an upright. He fell to the ground. The thing was the work of an instant. He was ascending jubilantly towards the sky: the same second he was lying on the ground. Doris did not realise what had happened. She had been envying him the ease with which he swung himself, the height of his ascent. She did not understand why he had stopped so suddenly. She perceived how still he seemed, half wondering.

'Charlie!' His silence frightened her. Her voice sank. 'Charlie!' She became angry. 'Why don't you answer me?' She moved closer to him, observing in what an ugly heap he lay. 'Charlie!'

Yet he vouchsafed her no reply. He lay so still. It was such an unusual thing for Charlie to be still, the strangeness of it began to get upon her nerves. Her face clouded. She was making ready to rush off and alarm the house in an agony of weeping. Already she was starting, when Someone came to her from across the lawn, and laid His hand upon her shoulder.

'Doris, what is wrong?'

The voice was a stranger's, and the presence. But she paid no heed to that: all her thoughts were concentrated on a single theme.

'Charlie!' she gasped.

'What ails Charlie?'

The Stranger, kneeling beside the silent boy, bent over him, gently turning him so that He could see his face. Then, raising him from the ground, gathering him in His arms, He held him to His breast; and, stooping, He whispered in his ear:

'Wake up, Charlie! Doris wants you.'

And the boy sat up, and looked in the face of Him in whose arms he was.

'Hollo!' he said. 'Who are you?'

'The friend of little children.'

There was an appreciable space of time before the answer came, and when it did come it was accompanied by a smile, as the Stranger looked the boy straight in the eyes. The boy laughed outright.

'I like the look of you.'

Doris drew a little nearer. She had her fingers to her lips, seeming more than half afraid.

'Charlie, I thought you were hurt.'

'Hurt!' he flashed at her; then back at the Stranger: 'I'm not hurt, am I?'

'No, you are not hurt; you are well, and whole, and strong.'

'But you tumbled from the swing.' The boy stared at Doris as if he thought she must be dreaming. 'The swing broke.'

'Broke?' Glancing up, he perceived the severed rope. 'Why, so it has.'

'It can soon be mended.'

The Stranger put the boy down, and went to the swing, and in a moment the two ends of the rope were joined together. Then He lifted them both on the seat, the boy and the girl together—there was ample room for both—and swung them gently to and fro. And as He swung He talked to them, and they to Him.

And when they had had enough of swinging He went with them, hand in hand, and sat with them on the grass by the side of the lake, with the trees at their back. And again He talked to them, and they to Him. And the simple things of which He spoke seemed strange to them, and wonderful. Never had anyone talked to them like that before. They kept as close to Him as they could, and put their arms about Him so far as they were able, and nestled their faces against His side, and they were happy.

While the Stranger and the children still conversed together there came down through the woods, towards the lake, a lady and a gentleman. He was a tall man, and held himself very straight, speaking as if he were very much in earnest.

'Doris, why should we keep on pretending to each other? I know that you love me, and you know that I love you. Why should you spoil your life—and mine!—for the sake of such a hound?'

'He is my husband.'

She spoke a little below her breath, as if she were ashamed of the fact. He struck impatiently at the bracken with his stick.

'Your husband! That creature! As though it were not profanation to link you with such an animal.'

'And then there are the children.'

Her voice sank lower, as if this time she spoke of something sacred. He noted the difference in the intonation; apparently he resented it. He struck more vigorously at the bracken, as if actuated by a desire to relieve his feelings. There was an interval, during which both of them were silent. Then he turned to her with sudden passion.

'Doris, come with me, at once! now! Give yourself to me, and I'll devote my whole life to you. You've known enough of me through all these things to be sure that you can trust me. Aren't you sure that you can trust me?'

'Yes, I am sure that I can trust you—in a sense.'

Something in her face seemed to make an irresistible appeal to him. He took her in his arms, she offering no resistance.

'In a sense? In what sense? Can't you trust me in every sense?'

'I can trust you to be true to me; but I am not so sure that I can trust you to let me be true to myself.'

'What hair-splitting's this? I'll let you be true to your own womanhood; it's you who shirk. You seem to want me to treat you as if you were an automatic figure, not a creature of flesh and blood. I can't do it—you can't trust me to do it; that thing's plain. Come, darling, let's take the future in our own hands, and together wrest happiness from life. You know that at my side you'll be content. See how you're trembling! There's proof of it. I'll swear I'll be content at yours! Come, Doris, come!'

'Where will you take me?'

'That's not your affair just now. I'll take you where I will. All you have to do is—come.'

She drew herself out of his arms, and a little away from him. She put up her hand as if to smooth her hair, he watching her with eager eyes.

'I'll come.'

He took her again in his embrace, softly, tenderly, as if she were some fragile, priceless thing. His voice trembled.

'You darling! When?'

'Now. Since all's over, and everything's to begin again, the sooner a beginning's made the better.' A sort of rage came into her voice—a note of hysteric pain. 'If you're to take me, take me as I am, in what I stand. I dare say he'll send my clothes on after me—and my jewels, perhaps.'

It seemed as if her tone troubled him, as if he endeavoured to soothe her.

'Don't talk like that, Doris. Everything that you want I'll get you—all that your heart can desire.'

'Except peace of mind!'

'I trust that I shall be able to get you even that. Only come!'

'Don't I tell you that I am ready? Why don't you start?'

He appeared to find her manner disconcerting. He searched her face, as if to discover if she were in earnest, then looked at his watch.

'If we make haste across the park, we shall be able to catch the express to town.'

'Then let's make haste and catch it.'

'Come!'

They began to walk quickly, side by side. As they passed round the bend they came on the two children sitting, with the Stranger, beside the lake. The children, scrambling to their feet, came running to them.

'Mamma,' they cried, 'come and see the friend of little children!'

At sight of them the woman drew back, as if afraid. The man interposed.

'Don't worry, you youngsters! Your mother's in a hurry—run away! Come, Doris, make haste; we've no time to lose if we wish to catch the train.'

He put his arm through hers, and made as if to draw her past them. She seemed disposed to linger.

'Let me—say good-bye to them.'

He whispered in her ear:

'There'll only be a scene; don't be foolish, child! There's not a moment to lose!' He turned angrily to the boy and girl. 'Don't you hear, you youngsters!—run away!' As the children moved aside, frightened at his violence, and bewildered by the strangeness of their mother's manner, he gripped the woman's arm more firmly, beginning by sheer force to hurry her off. 'Come, Doris,' he exclaimed, 'don't be an idiot!'

The Stranger, who had been sitting on the grass, stood up and faced them.

'Rather be wise. There still is time. What is it you would do?'

The interruption took the pair completely by surprise. The man stared angrily at the Stranger.

'Who are you, sir? And what do you mean by interfering in what is no concern of yours?'

'Are you sure that it is no concern of Mine?'

The man endeavoured to meet the Stranger's eyes, with but scant success. His erect, bold, defiant attitude gave place to one of curious uncertainty.

'How can it be any concern of yours?'

'All things are My concern, the things which you do, and the things which you leave undone. Would it were not so, for many and great are the burdens which you lay upon me. You wicked man! Yet more foolish even than wicked! What is this woman to you that you should seek to slay her body and soul? Is she not of those who know not what is the thing they do till it is done? It is well with you if this sin, also, shall not be laid to your charge,—that you are a blind leader of the blind!'

The Stranger turned to the woman.

'Your eyes shall be opened. Look upon this man to see him as he is.'

The woman looked at the man. As she looked, a change came over him. Before her accusatory glance he seemed to dwindle and wax old. He grew ugly, his jaw dropped open, his eyes were full of lust, cruelty was writ upon his countenance. On a sudden he had become a thing of evil. She shrank back with a cry of horror and alarm, while he stood before her cowering like some guilty creature whose shame has been suddenly made plain. And the Stranger said to him:

'Go! and seek that peace of which you would have robbed her.'

The man, shambling away round the bend in the path, presently was lost to sight. The Stranger was left alone with the children and the woman. The woman stood before Him trembling, with bowed form and face cast down, and she cried:

'Who are you, sir?'

The Stranger replied:

'Look upon Me: and as you knew the man, so, also, you shall know Me.'

She looked on Him, and knew Him, and wept.

'Lord, I know You! Have mercy upon me!'

He answered:

'I am the friend of little children, and of the mothers that bare them; for the pains of the women are not little ones; and because they are great, so also shall great mercy be shown unto them. For unto those that suffer most, shall not most be forgiven? for is not suffering akin to repentance?'

And the woman cried:

'Lord, I am not worthy Thy forgiveness!'

And to her He said:

'Is any worthy? No, not one. Yet many are those to whom forgiveness comes. There are your children, that are an heritage to you of God. Take them, and as you are unto them, so shall God be unto you, and more. Return to your husband; say to him what things have happened unto you, and fear not because of him.'

And the woman went, holding a child by either hand. And the Stranger stood and watched them as they went. And when they had gone some distance, the woman turned and looked at Him. And He called to her:

'Be of good courage!'

And after that she saw Him no more.

Chapter V

The students crowded the benches. Some wore hats and gloves, and carried sticks or umbrellas; they had the appearance of having just dropped in to enjoy a little passing relaxation. Others, hatless and gloveless, wore instead an air of intense preoccupation; they had note-books in their hands, and spent the time studying anatomical charts in sombre-covered volumes. Many were smoking pipes for the most part; the air was heavy with tobacco smoke. Nearly everybody talked; there was a continual clatter of voices; men on one side called to men on the other, exchanging jokes and laughter.

In the well below were the tables for the operator and his paraphernalia. Assistants were making all things ready. The smell of antiseptic fluids mingled with the odour of tobacco. Omnipresent was the pungent suggestion of carbolic acid. A glittering array of instruments was being sterilised and placed in order for the operator's hand. The anæsthetists were busy with their preparations to expedite unconsciousness, the dressers with their bandages to be applied when the knives had made an end.

There was about the whole theatre, and in particular about the little array of men upon the floor in their white shrouds, who were occupied in doing things the meaning of which was hidden from the average layman, something which the unaccustomed eye and ear and stomach would have found repulsive. But in the bearing of those who were actually present there was no hint that the work in which they were to be engaged had about it any of the elements of the disagreeable. They were, taking them all in all, and so far as appearances went, a careless, lighthearted, jovial crew.

When the operator entered, accompanied by two colleagues, there was silence, or, rather, a distinct hush. Pipes were put out, men settled in their seats, note-books were opened, opera-glasses were produced. The operator was a man of medium height and slender build, with slight side-whiskers and thin brown hair, which was turning gray. He wore spectacles. Having donned the linen duster, he turned up his shirtsleeves close to his shoulders, and with bare arms began to examine the preparations which the assistants had made. He glanced at the instruments, commented on the bandages, gave some final directions to an irrigator; then each man fell into his place and waited. The door opened and a procession entered. A stretcher was carried in by two men, one at the head and one at the foot. A nurse walked by the side, holding the patient by the hand; two other nurses accompanied. The patient was lifted on to the table. The porters, with the stretcher, withdrew. The nurse who had held the patient's hand stooped and kissed her, whispering words of comfort. The operator bent also. What he said was clearly audible.

'Don't be afraid; it will be all right.'

The patient said nothing. She was a woman of about thirty years, and was suffering from cancer in the womb.

Anæsthetics were applied, but she took them badly, fighting, struggling against their influence, crying and whimpering all the time. Force had to be used to restrain her movements on the table. When she felt their restraining hands, she began to be hysterical and to scream. A second attempt was made to bring about unconsciousness; again without result. The surgeons held a hurried consultation as to whether the operation should be carried out with the patient still in possession of her senses. It was resolved that there should be a third and more drastic effort to produce anæsthesia. On that occasion the desired result was brought about. Her cries and struggles ceased; she was in a state of torpor.

The body was bared; the knife began its work. . . .

The operation was not wholly successful. There had been fears that it would fail; but as, if it were not attempted, an agonising death would certainly ensue, it had been felt that it was a case in which every possible chance should be taken advantage of, and in which the undoubted risk was worth incurring. The woman was still young. She had a husband who loved her and children whom she loved. She did not wish to die; so it had been decided that surgical science should do its best to win life for her.

But it appeared that the worst fears on her account were likely to be realised. The operation was a prolonged one. The resistance she had offered to the application of the anæsthetics had weakened her. Soon after the surgeon began his labours it became obvious to those who knew him best that he had grave doubts as to what would be the issue. As he continued, his doubts grew more; they were exchanged for certainties, until it began to be whispered through the theatre that the operation, which was being brought to as rapid a conclusion as possible, was being conducted on a subject who was already dead.

The woman had died under the surgeon's knife. Shortly the fact was established beyond the possibility of challenge. Reagents of every kind were applied in the most effective possible manner; medical skill and experience did its utmost; but neither the Materia Medica nor the brains of doctors shall prevail against death, and this woman was already dead.

When the thing was made plain, there came into the atmosphere a peculiar quality. The students were very still; they neither moved nor spoke, but sat stiffly, with their eyes fixed on the naked woman extended on the oilskin pad. Some of those faces were white, their features set and rigid. This was notably the case with those who were youngest and most inexperienced, though there were those among the seniors who were ill at ease. It was almost as if they had been assisting at a homicide; before their eyes they had seen this woman done to death. The operator was a man whose nerve was notorious, or he would not have held the position which he did; but even he seemed to have been nonplussed by what had happened beneath his knife. His assistants clustered together, eyeing him askance, and each other, and the woman, with the useless bandages hiding the gaping wound. His colleagues whispered apart. They and he were all drabbled with blood; each seemed conscious of his ensanguined hands. All in the building had come full of faith in the man whose fame as a surgeon was a byword; it was as though their faith had received an ugly jar.

While the hush endured, One rose from His place on the benches, and stepping on to the operating floor, moved towards the woman. An assistant endeavoured to interpose.

'Go back to your place, sir. What do you mean by coming here?'

'You have done your work. Am I not, then, to do Mine?'

The assistant stared, taken aback by what seemed to him to be impudence.

'Don't talk nonsense! Who are you, sir?'

'I am He you know not of—a help to those in pain.'

The assistant hesitated, glancing from the Speaker to his chief. The Stranger drew a sheet over the woman, so that only her face remained uncovered. Turning to the operator, He beckoned with His finger.

'Come!'

The surgeon went. The Stranger said to him, pointing towards the woman:

'Insomuch as what you have done was done for her, it is well; insomuch as it was done for your own advancing, it was ill. Yet be not afraid. Blessed are the hands which heal men's wounds, and wipe the tears of pain out of their eyes. Better to be of use to those that suffer than to be a king. For the time shall come when you shall say: "As I did unto others, so do, Lord, unto me." And it shall be done. Yet do it, not for the swelling of your purse, but for your brother's sake, and your payment shall be of God.'

And the Stranger, turning, spoke to the students on the benches; and their eyes never moved from Him as, wondering, they listened to His words.

'Hearken, O young men, while I speak to you of the things which your fathers have forgotten, and would not remember if they could. You would go forth as healers of men? It is well. Go forth! Heal! The world is very sick. Women labour; men sigh because of their pains. But, physicians, heal first yourselves. Be sure that you go forth in the spirit of healing. Where there is suffering, there go; ask not why it comes, nor whence, nor what shall be the fee. Heal only. The labourer is worthy of his hire; yet it is not for his hire he should labour. Heal for the healing's sake, and because of the pain which is in the world. God shall measure out to the physician his appointed fee. Trouble not yourselves with that. The less your gain, the greater your gain. There is One that keeps count. Each piece of money you heap upon the other lessens your store. I tell you that there is joy in heaven each time a sufferer is eased, at his brother's hands, of pain, because it was his brother.'

When the Stranger ceased, the students looked from him at each other. They began to murmur among themselves.

'Who is this fellow?'

'What does he mean by preaching at us?'

'Inflicting on us a string of platitudes!'

And one, bolder than the rest, called out:

'Yours is excellent advice, sir, but in the light of what's just occurred it seems hardly to the point. Couldn't you demonstrate instead of talk?'

The Stranger looked in the direction from which the voice came.

'Stand up!'

The student stood up. He was a young man of about twenty-four, with a shrewd, earnest face. In his hand he held an open note-book.

'Always the world seeks for a sign; without a sign it will not believe—nor with a sign. What demonstration would you have of Me?'

'Are you a doctor, sir?'

'I am a healer of men.'

'With what degree?'

'One you know not of.'

'Yet I thought I knew something of all degrees.'

'Not all. Young man, you will find the world easy, heaven hard. Yet because there are many here like unto you, I will show to you a sign; exhibit My degree.'

The Stranger turned to the operating surgeon.

'You say that the woman whom you sought to heal is dead?'

'Beyond a doubt, unfortunately.'

'You are sure?'

'Certain.'

'Of that you are all persuaded?'

Again there came murmurs from the students on the benches:

'What's he up to?'

'Who's he getting at?'

'Throw him out!'

The Stranger waited till the murmuring was at an end. Then He turned to the woman, and, stooping, kissed her on the lips.

'Daughter!' He said.

And, behold, the woman sat up and looked about her.

'Where am I?' she asked, as one who wakes from sleep.

'Is all well with you?'

'Oh, yes, all's well with me, thank God!'

'That is good hearing.'

Then there was a tumult in the theatre. The students stood up in their places, speaking all together.

'How's he done it?'

'She must have been only shamming.'

'It's a trick!'

'It's a plant!'

'It's a got-up thing between them.'

Insults were hurled at the Stranger by a hundred different voices. In the heat of their excitement the students came streaming down from their seats on to the operating floor. They looked for the man who had done this thing.

'Where is he?' they cried. 'We'll make him confess how the trick was done.'

But He whom they sought was not there. He had already gone. When they discovered that this was so, and that He whom they sought was not to be found, but had vanished from before their eyes, their bewilderment grew still more. With one accord they turned to look at the woman.

As if alarmed by the noise of their threatening voices, and the confusion caused by their tumultuous movements, she had raised herself upon the operating table, so that she stood upright before them all, naked as she was born. And they saw that the bandages had fallen from off her, and that her body was without scratch and blemish, round and whole.

'It's a miracle!' they exclaimed.

A great silence fell over them all, until, presently, the surgeons and the students, looking each into the other's faces, began to ask, each of his neighbour:

'Who is the man that has done this thing?'

But the woman gave thanks unto God, weeping tears of joy.

Chapter VI

The Blackleg

The foreman shrugged his shoulders. He avoided looking at the applicant, an undersized man, with straggling black beard and dull eyes. Even now, while pressing his appeal, he wore an air of being but slightly interested.

'You know, Jones, what the conditions of employ were—keep on the works.'

'But my little girl's ill!'

'Sorry to hear it; but you don't want to have any trouble. You heard how they treated your wife when she came in; they'd be much worse to you if I was to let you out. They're pretty near beat, and they know it, and they don't like it, and before they quite knock under they'd like to make a mark of someone. If it was you, they might make a mark too many; they're not overfond of you just now, as you know very well. And then where will you be, eh? How would your little girl be any better for their laying you out?'

Jones turned to his wife, a sort of feminine replica of himself. She had her shawl drawn over her head.

'You hear, Jane, what Mr. Mason says?'

Mrs. Jones sighed; even in her sigh there was a curious reproduction of her husband's lack of interest.

'All I know is that the doctor don't seem to have no great 'opes about Matilda, and that she keeps a-calling for you, Tom.'

'Does she? Then I go! Mr. Mason, I'm a-goin'.'

'All right, Jones, go! Don't think that I don't feel for yer, 'cause I do, but as to coming back again, that's another matter. Mind, we can do without yer, and we don't want no fuss, that's all. Things have been bad enough up to now, and we don't want 'em to be no worse.'

Outside the gates there was a considerable crowd. Among the crowd were the pickets and a fair leaven of the men on strike; but a large majority of the people might have been described as sympathisers. Unwise sympathisers they for the most part were; more bent on striking than the strikers; more resolute to fight the battle to the bitter end. The knowledge that already surrender was in the air angered them. They were in an ugly temper, disposed to 'take it out of' the first most convenient object.

As Mrs. Jones had made her way through them towards the gates she had been subjected to gibes and jeers, and worse. She had been pushed and hustled. More than one hand had been laid rudely on her. Someone had thrown a shovelful of dirt with such adroitness that it had burst in a shower on her head. While she was still nearly blinded she had been pushed hither and thither with half good-humoured horse-play, which was near akin to something else.

Tom Jones was an unpopular figure. He was one of the most notorious of the blacklegs, in a sense their leader. He had persisted in being master of his own volition; asserted his right to labour for whom he pleased, at whatever terms he chose. Such men are the greatest enemies of trades unions. Allow a man his freedom, and unionism, in its modern sense, is at an end. It is one of the questions of the moment whether the good of the greatest number does not imperatively demand special legislation which shall hold such men in bonds; which shall make it a penal offence for them to consider themselves free.

Word had gone round that Jones's little girl was ill; that the doctor had decided she was dying; that Mrs. Jones had come to fetch him home to bid the child good-bye. By most of those there it was unhesitatingly agreed that this was as it should be; that Jones was being served just right; that he was only getting a bit of what he ought to have, which, it was quite within the range of possibility, they would supplement with something else.

It was because of Jones and his like that the strike was failing, had failed; that they were beaten and broken, brought to their knees, in spite of all their organisation, of what they had endured. Jones! It was currently reported that the idea of giving the blacklegs food and lodging on the premises, and so rendering the wiles of the pickets of no avail, was Jones's. At any rate, he had been among the first to fall in with the proposition, and for many days he had not been outside the gates. Jones! Let him put his face outside those gates now and he would see what they would show him.

When the gates were opened, and Mrs. Jones had entered, they waited, murmuring and muttering, with twitching fingers and lowering brows, wondering if the prospect of being able to bid his dying child good-bye would be sufficient inducement to him to trust himself outside there in the open. And while they wondered he came.

Again the gate was opened. Out came Jones; close behind him was his wife. Then the gate was shut to with a bang.

He was known by sight to many in the crowd. By them the knowledge of who he was was instantly communicated to all the rest. He was not greeted with any tumult; they were too much in earnest to be noisy. But, with one accord, they cursed him, and their curses, though not loudly uttered, reached him, every one. He stood fronting the array of angry faces, all inclined in his direction.

The three policemen, who kept a clear space in front of the works, and saw that ingress and egress was gained with some sort of ease, hardly seemed to know what to make of him, or of the situation. They glanced at Jones, then at the crowd, then at each other. All the morning the people had been gathering round the gate, the number increasing as the minutes passed. Except that they could not be induced to move away, there had been little to object to in their demeanour until now. As Jones appeared with his wife they formed together into a more compact mass. Another shovelful of dust was thrown by someone at the back with the same dexterity as before, so that it lighted on the man and the woman, partially obscuring them beneath a cloud of dust. That same instant perhaps a dozen stones were thrown, some of which struck both Mr. and Mrs. Jones, the rest rattling against the gate.

It was done so quickly that the police had not a chance to offer interference. They had been instructed to make as little show of authority as possible, to bear as much as could be borne, and, until the last extremity, to do nothing to rouse the rancour of the strikers. In the face of this sudden assault the trio hesitated. Then the one nearest to the gate held his hand up to the crowd, shouting:

'Now, you chaps, none of that! Don't you go making fools of yourselves, or you'll be sorry!' He turned to the Joneses. 'You'd better go back and try to get out some other way. There'll be trouble if you stop here.'

Tom Jones asked him stolidly, gazing with his lack-lustre eyes intently at the crowd:

'Which other way?'

'I don't know—any other way. You can't get this way, that's plain—they mean mischief. Back you go, before you're sorry.'

The constable endeavoured to hustle the pair back within the gate. But Jones would not have it.

'My child's dying; this is the nearest way to her. I'm going this way.'

The officer persisted in his attempt to persuade him to change his mind.

'Don't be silly! You won't do your child any good by getting yourself knocked to pieces, will you?'

Tom Jones was obstinate.

'I'm going this way.'

Slipping past the constable, he moved towards the crowd. The people confronted him like a solid wall.

'Let me pass, you chaps.'

That moment the storm broke. The man's stolid demeanour, the complete indifference with which he faced their rage, might have had something to do with it. The effect of his request to be allowed to pass was as if he had dropped a lighted match into a powder-magazine. An explosion followed. The air was rent by curses; the people became all at once like madmen. Possessed with sudden frenzy, they crowded round the man, raining on him a hail of blows, each man struggling with his fellow in order to reach the object of his rage. Their very fury defeated their purpose. Not a few of the blows which were meant for Jones fell on their own companions. With the commencement of the attack Jones's stolidity completely vanished. He was transformed into a fiend, and behaved like one. His voice was heard above the others, pouring forth a flood of objurgations on the heads of his assailants. His wife was his slavish disciple. Her shrill tones were mingled with his deeper ones; they were at least as audible. Her language was no better, her passion was no less. The man and the woman fought like wild beasts. And so blinded by fury were the efforts of their assailants that the pair were able to give back much more than they received.

The attempts of the police at pacification were useless. They were not in sufficient force. And there is a point in the temper of a crowd at which its rage is not to be appeased until it has vented itself on the object of its fury. All that the officers succeeded in doing was to lose their own tempers. Under certain circumstances there is irresistible contagion in a madman's frenzy. Presently they themselves were mingling in the frantic mêlée, apparently with as little show of reason as the rest.

Suddenly the crowd gave way towards the centre. Those in the middle were borne down by those who persisted in pressing on. There was a struggling, heaving, mouthing mass upon the ground, with the Joneses underneath. And, as the writhings and contortions of this heap grew less and less, there came One, before whose touch men gave way, so that, before they knew it, He stood there, in their very midst, before them all. In His presence their rage was stilled. Ceasing to contend, they drew back, looking towards Him with their bloodshot eyes. Where had been the pile of living men was a clear space, in which He stood. At His feet were two forms—Tom Jones and his wife. The woman cried and groaned, twisting her limbs; but the man lay still.

'What is it that you would do?'

With the sorrowful inflexion of the voice was blended a satiric intonation which seemed to strike some of those who heard as with a thong. One man, a big, burly fellow, chose to take the question as addressed to himself. He still trembled with excess of rage; his voice was husky; from his mouth there came a volley of oaths.

'Bash the — to a jelly—that's what we'd like to do to his — carcase! It's through the likes of him that our homes are broken up, our kids starving, our wives with pretty near nothing on. Killing's too good for such a—!'

'Who are you that you should judge your brother?'

The man spat on the pavement.

'He's no brother of mine—not much he ain't! If I'd a brother like him, I'd cut my throat!'

'Since all men are brethren, and this is a man, if he is not your brother, what, then, are you?'

'He's no man! If he is, I hope I ain't.'

The Stranger was for a moment silent, looking at the speaker, who, drawing the back of his hand across his mouth, averted his glance.

'You are a man—as he is. Would that you both were more than men, or less. Go, all of you that would shed innocent blood, knowing not what it is you do. Wash the stain from off your hands; for if your hands are clean, so also are your hearts. As your ignorance is great, so also is God's mercy. Go, I say, and learn who is your brother.'

And the people went, slinking off, for the most part, in little groups of threes and fours, muttering together. Some there were who made haste, and ran, thinking that the man was dead, and fearful of what might follow.

When they were all gone, the Stranger turned to the woman, who still cried and made a noise.

'Cease, woman, and go to your daughter, lest she be dead before you come.'

And stooping, he touched the man upon the shoulder, saying:

'Rise!'

And the man stood up, and the Stranger said to him:

'Haste, and go to your daughter, who calls for you continually.'

And the man and the woman went away together, without a word.

Chapter VII

In Piccadilly

It was past eleven. The people, streaming out of the theatres, poured into Piccadilly Circus. The night was fine, so that those on foot were disposed to take their time. The crowd was huge, its constituent parts people of all climes and countries, of all ranks and stations. To the unaccustomed eye the confusion was bewildering; omnibuses rolled heavily in every direction; hansom cabs made efforts to break through what, to the eyes of their sanguine drivers, seemed breaks in the line of traffic; carriages filled with persons in evening-dress made such haste as they could. The pavements were crowded almost to the point of danger; even in the roadway foot-passengers passed hither and thither amidst the throng of vehicles, while on every side vendors of evening papers pushed and scrambled, shouting out, with stentorian lungs, what wares they had to sell.

The papers met with a brisk demand. Strange tales were told in them. Readers were uncertain as to the light in which they ought to be regarded; editors were themselves in doubt as to the manner in which it would be proper to set them forth. Some wrote in a strain which was intended to be frankly humorous; others told the stories baldly, leaving readers to take them as they chose; while still a third set did their best to dish them up in the shape of a wild sensation.

It was currently reported that a Mysterious Stranger had appeared in London. During the last few hours He had been seen by large numbers of people. The occasions on which He had created the most remarkable impressions had been two. At St. John's Hall the Rev. Philip Evans had been preaching on the Second Coming, when, in the middle of the discourse, a Stranger had appeared upon the platform, actually claiming, so far as could be gathered, to be the Christ. In the operating theatre at St. Philip's Hospital, just as a subject—a woman—had succumbed under the surgeon's knife, a Stranger had come upon the scene, and, before all eyes, had restored the dead to life. It was this story of the miracle, as it was called, at St. Philip's Hospital, which had been exciting London all that day. The thing was incredible; but the witnesses were so reputable, their statements so emphatic, the details given so precise, it was difficult to know what to make of it. And now in the evening papers there was a story of how a riot had taken place outside Messrs. Anthony's works. The strikers had attacked a blackleg. A stranger had come upon them while they were in the very thick of the fracas; at a word from Him the tumult ceased; before His presence the brawlers had scattered like chaff before the wind. The latest editions were full of the tale; it was in everybody's mouth.

Christ's name was in the air, the topic of the hour. The Stranger's claim was, of course, absurd, unspeakable. He was an impostor, some charlatan; at best, a religious maniac. Similar creatures had arisen before, notably in the United States, though we had not been without them here in England, and Roman Catholic countries had had their share. The story of the dead woman who had been restored to life at St. Philip's Hospital was odd, but it was capable of natural explanation. To doubt this would be to write one's self down a lunatic, a superstitious fool, a relic of medieval ignorance. There is no going outside natural laws; the man who pretends to do so writes himself down a knave, and pays those to whom he appeals a very scanty compliment. Why, even the most pious of God's own ministers have agreed that there are no miracles, and never have been. Go to with your dead woman restored to life!

Yet, the tale was an odd one, especially as it was so well attested. But then the thing was so well done that it seemed that those present were in a state of mind in which they would have been prepared to swear to anything.

Still, Christ's name was in the air—in an unusual sense. It came from unaccustomed lips. Even the women of the pavement spoke of Jesus, wondering if there was such a man, and what would happen if He were to come again.

'Suppose this fellow in the papers turned out to be Him, how would that be then?' one inquired of the other. Then both were silent, for they were uneasy; and at the first opportunity they solaced themselves with a drink.

The men for the most part were more outspoken in ribaldry than the women, especially those specimens of masculinity who frequented at that hour the purlieus of Piccadilly Circus. Common-sense was their stand-by. What was not in accordance with the teachings of common-sense was nothing. How could it be otherwise? Judged by this standard, the tales which were told were nonsense, sheer and absolute. Therefore, in so far as they were concerned, the scoffer's was the proper mental attitude. The editors who wrote of them humorously were the level-headed men. They were only fit to be laughed at.

'If I'd been at St. Philip's, I'd have got hold of that very mysterious stranger, and I'd have kept hold until I'd got from him an explanation of that pretty little feat of hanky-panky.'

The speaker was standing at the Piccadilly corner of the Circus, by the draper's shop. He was a tall man, and held a cigar in his mouth. His overcoat was open, revealing the evening dress beneath. The man to whom he spoke was shorter. He was dressed in tweeds; his soft felt hat, worn a little on one side of his head, lent to him a mocking air. When the other spoke, he laughed.

'I'd like to have a shy at him myself. I've seen beggars of his sort in India, where they do a lot of mischief, sometimes sending whole districts stark staring mad. But there they do believe in them; thank goodness we don't!'

'How do you make that out, when you read the names of the people who are prepared to swear to the truth of the St. Philip's tale?'

'My dear boy, long before this they're sorry. Fellows lost their heads—sort of moment of delirium, which will leave a bad taste in their mouths now they've got well out of it. If that mysterious gentleman ever comes their way again, they'll be every bit as ready to keep a tight hold of him as you could be.'

'I wonder.' The tall man puffed at his cigar. 'I'd give—well, Grey, I won't say how much, but I'd give a bit to have him stand in front of me just here and now. That kind of fellow makes me sick. The common or garden preacher I don't mind; he has his uses. But the kind of creature who tries to trade on the folly of the great majority, by trying to make out that he's something which he isn't—whenever he's about there ought to be a pump just handy. We're too lenient to cattle of his particular breed.'

'Suppose, Boyle, this mysterious stranger were to appear in Piccadilly now, what's the odds that you, for one, wouldn't try to plug him in the eye?'

'I don't know about me, but I'm inclined to think that there are others who would endeavour their little best to reach him thereabouts. Piccadilly at this time of night is hardly the place for a mysterious anyone to cut a figure to much advantage. I fancy there'd be ructions. Anyhow, I'd like to see him come.'

Mr. Boyle's tone was grim. His companion laughed; but before the sound of his laughter had long died out the speaker's wish was gratified.

All in an instant, without any sort of warning, there was one of those scenes which occur in Piccadilly on most nights of the week. A woman had been drinking; she was young, new to her trade, still unaccustomed to the misuse of stimulants. She made a noise. A female acquaintance endeavoured to induce her to go away; in vain. The girl, pulling up her skirts, began to dance and shout, and to behave like a virago, among the throng of loiterers who were peopling the pavement. A man made some chaffing remark to her. She flew at him like a tiger-cat. Directly there was an uproar. There are times and seasons when it requires but a very little thing to transform those midnight Saturnalia into chaos. The police hurled themselves into the struggling throng, making captives of practically everyone on whom they could lay their hands.

The crowd was in uncomfortable proximity to Mr. Grey and his friend. It swayed in their direction.

'We'd better clear out of this, Boyle, before there's an ugly rush comes our way. Let's get across the road. I'm in no humour for skittles to-night, if you don't mind.'

The speaker glanced smilingly towards the seething throng. It was the humorous side of the thing which appealed to him; he had seen it so often before. Boyle diverted his attention.

'Hollo! who's this?'

Someone stepped from the roadway on to the pavement, moving quickly, yet lightly, so that there was about His actions no appearance of haste. He held His hands a little raised. People made way to let Him pass, as if they knew that He was coming, even though He approached them in silence from behind.

'It's Christ!'

The exclamation was Grey's reply to his friend's query. Boyle, starting, turned to stare at him.

'Grey, what do you mean?'

'It's Christ! Don't you know Christ when you see him? It's the mysterious stranger! Why don't you go and lay fast hold on him?'

Boyle stared at his friend in silence. There was that in his manner which was disconcerting—an obsession. The fashion of his face was changed; a new light was in his eyes. The big man seemed half amused, half startled. As he stood and listened and watched, his amusement diminished, his appearance of being startled grew.

The crowd had given way before the Stranger, making a lane through which He had passed to its midst; and it was silent. The vehicles rumbled along the road; from the other side of the street the voices of newsboys assailed the air; pedestrians went ceaselessly to and fro; but there, where the noise had just been greatest, all was still—a strange calm had come on the excited throng.

There were there all sorts and conditions of men and women that had fallen away from virtue. There were men of all ages, from white haired to beardless boys; from those who had drained the cup of vice to its uttermost dregs, yet still clutched with frantic, trembling fingers at the empty goblet, to those who had just begun to peep over its edge, and to feast their eyes on its fulness to the brim. There were men of all stations, from old and young rakes of fortune and family to struggling clerks, shop-assistants, office-boys, and those creatures of the gutter who rake the kennels for offal with which to fill their bellies. Among the women there was the same diversity. They were of all nations—English, French, German, and the rest; of all ages—grandmothers and girls who had not yet attained to the age of womanhood. There were some of birth and breeding, and there were daughters of the slums, heritors of their mothers' foulness. There were the comparatively affluent, and there were those who had gone all day hungry, and who still looked for a stroke of fortune to gain for them a night's lodging. But they all were the same; they all had painted faces, and they all were decked in silks and satins or such other tawdry splendour as by any crooked means they could lay their hands on which would serve to advertise their trade.

And in the midst of this assemblage of the dregs of humanity the Stranger stood; and He put to them the question which was to become familiar ere long to not a few of the people of the city:

'What is it you would do?'

They returned no answer; instead, they looked at Him askance, doubt, hesitancy, surprise, wonder, awe, revealing themselves in varying degrees upon their faces as they were seen beneath the paint.

Two policemen had in custody the young woman who had been the original cause of disturbance. Each held her by an arm. The Stranger turned to them.

'Loose her.'

Without an attempt at remonstrance they did as He bade. They took their hands from off her and set her free. She stood before them, seeming ashamed and sobered, with downcast face, seeking the pavement with her eyes. But all at once, as if she could not bear the silence any longer, she raised her head and met His glance, asking:

'Who are you?'

'Do you not know Me?'

'Know you?'

Her tone suggested that she was searching her memory to recall His face.

'If you do not know Me now that you look on Me, then shall I never be known to you. Yet it is strange that it should be so, for I am the Friend of sinners.'

'The Friend—'

The girl got so far in repeating the Strangers words, then suddenly stopped, and, bursting into a passion of tears, threw herself on her knees on the pavement at His feet crying:

'Lord, I know You! Have mercy upon me!'

The Stranger touched her with His hand.

'In that you know Me it shall be well with you.'

He looked about him on the crowd.

'Would that you all knew Me, even as this woman does!'

But the people eyed each other, wondering. There were some who laughed, and others inquired among themselves:

'Who is this fellow? And what is the matter with the girl, that she goes on like this?'

One there was who cried:

'Tell us who you are.'

'I am He that you know not of.'

'That's all right, so far as it goes, but it doesn't go far enough; it's an insufficient definition. What's your name?'

'Day and night you call upon My name, yet do not know Me.'

'Look here, my friend; are you suggesting that you're anybody in particular? because, if so, tell us straight out, who? We're not good at conundrums, and at this time of night it's not fair to start us solving them.'

The Stranger was silent. His gaze passed eagerly from face to face. When He had searched them all, He cried:

'Is there not one that knows Me save this woman? Is there not one?'

A man came out from amidst the people, and stood in front of the Stranger.

'I know You,' he said. 'You are Christ.'

Chapter VIII

The Only One that was Left

Stillness followed the man's words until the people began to fidget, and to shuffle with their feet, and to murmur:

'What talk is this? What blasphemy does this man utter? Who is this mountebank to whom he speaks?'

But the Stranger continued to look at the man who had come out from the crowd. And He asked him:

'How is it that you know Me, since I do not know you?'

The man laughed, and, as he did so, it was seen that the Stranger started, and drew a little back.

'Because I know You, it doesn't follow that You should know me. I'd rather that You didn't. Directly You came into the street I knew that it was You, and wished You further. What do You want to trouble us for? Aren't we better off without You?'

The Stranger held up His hand as if to keep the other from Him.

'You thing all evil, return to your own kind!'

The man drew back into the crowd, a little uncertainly, as if crestfallen, but laughing all the time. He strode off down the street; they could still hear his laughter as he went. The Stranger, with the people, seemed to listen. As the sound grew fainter He cried to them with a loud voice:

'Save this woman and that man, is there none that knows Me? No, not one!'

The traffic had been brought almost to a standstill. The dimensions of the crowd had increased. There was a block of vehicles before it in the street. From the roof of an omnibus, which was crowded within and without with passengers, there came a shout as of a strong man:

'Lord, I know You! God be thanked that He has suffered me to see this day!'

The Stranger replied, stretching out His arms in the direction in which the speaker was:

'It is well with you, friend, and shall be better. Go, spread the tidings! Tell those that know Me that I am come!'

There came the answer back:

'Even so, Lord, I will do Your bidding; and in the city there shall rise the sound of a great song. Hark! I hear the angels singing!'

There came over the crowd's mood one of those sudden changes to which such heterogeneous gatherings are essentially liable. As question and answer passed to and fro, and the man's voice rose to a triumphal strain, the people began to be affected by a curious sense of excitation, asking of each other:

'Who, then, is this man? Is he really someone in particular? Perhaps he may be able to do something for us, or to give us something, if we ask him. Who knows?'

They began to press upon Him, men and women, old and young, rich and poor, each with a particular request of his or her own.

'Give us a trifle!'

'The price of a night's lodging!'

'A drop to drink!'

'A cab-fare!'

'Tell us who you are!'

'Give us a speech!'

'If you can do miracles, do one now!'

'Cure the lot of us!'

'Make us whole!'

The requests were of all sorts and kinds. The Stranger looked upon the throng of applicants with glances in which were both pity and pain.

'What I would give to you you will not have. What, then, is it that I shall give to you?'

There was a chorus in return. For every material want He was entreated to provide. He shook His head.

'Those things which you ask I cannot give; they are not Mine. I have not money, nor money's worth. There is none amongst you that is so poor as I am.'

'Then what can you give?'

'Those who would know what I can give must follow Me. The way is hard, and the journey long. At the end is the peace which is not of this world.'

'Where do you go?'

'Unto My Father.'

'Who is your father?'

'Those that know Me know also My Father.'

Turning as he spoke, He began to walk in the direction of Hyde Park. Some of the people, apparently supposing that His injunction to follow Him was to be understood in a literal sense, formed in a straggling band behind Him. At first there were not many. His movement, which was unexpected, had taken the bulk of the crowd by surprise. For some seconds it was not generally realised that He had commenced to pass away. When all became aware of what was happening, and it was understood that the mysterious Stranger was going from them, another wave of excitement passed through the throng, and something like a rush was made to keep within sight of Him. The farther they went, the greater became the number of those that went with Him. But it was observed that none came within actual touch. He walked with people in front, behind, on either side, yet alone. He occupied an empty space in their very midst, with no one within six or seven feet, moving neither quickly nor slowly, with head bowed, and hands hanging loose at His sides, seeming to see none of those that went with Him; and it was as though an unseen barrier was round about Him which even the more presumptuous of His attendants could not pass.

Along Piccadilly, past the shops, past Green Park, the procession went, growing larger and larger as it progressed. Persons, wondering what was the cause of the to-do, asked questions; then fell in with the others, curious to learn what the issue of the affair would be. Traffic in the road became congested. Vehicles could not proceed above a walking pace, because of the people who hemmed them in. Nor did their occupants, or their drivers, seem loath to linger with the throng. The police adapted their mood to that of the crowd. They saw men and women pouring out of restaurants and public-houses to join the Stranger's retinue, and were, for the most part, content to keep pace with it, keeping a watchful eye for what might be the possible upshot of the singular proceedings.

At Hyde Park Corner the Stranger stopped, and it could then be seen to what huge proportions the throng had grown. The whole open space was filled with people, and when, with the Stranger's, their advance was stayed, pedestrians and vehicles seemed mixed in inextricable confusion. Probably the large majority of those present had but the faintest notion of what had brought them there. In obedience to a sudden impulse of the gregarious instinct they had joined the crowd because the crowd was there to join.

As He stopped the Stranger raised His head, and looked about Him. He saw how large was the number of the people, and He said, in a voice which was only clearly audible to those who stood near:

'It is already late. Is it not time that you should go to your homes and rest?'

A man replied; he was a young fellow in evening dress; he had had more than enough to drink:

'It's early yet. You don't call this late! The evening's only just beginning! We're game to make a night of it if you are. Where you lead us we will follow.'

The young man's words were followed by a burst of laughter from some of those who heard. The Stranger sighed. Turning towards Hyde Park, He moved towards the open gates. The crowd opened to let Him pass, then closing in, it followed after. The Stranger entered the silent park. Crossing Rotten Row, He led the way to the grassy expanse which lay beyond. Not the whole crowd went with Him. The vehicles went their several ways, many also of the people. Some stayed, loitering and talking over what had happened; so far, that is, as they understood. These the police dispersed. Still, those who continued with the Stranger were not few.

When He reached the grass the Stranger stopped again. The people, gathering closer, surrounded Him, as if expecting Him to speak. But He was still. They looked at Him with an eager curiosity. At first He did not look at them at all. So that, while with their intrusive glances they searched Him, as it were, from head to foot, He stood in their midst with bent head and downcast eyes. They talked together, some in whispers, and some in louder tones; and there were some who laughed, until, at last, a man called out:

'Well, what have you brought us here for? To stand on the grass and catch cold?'

The Stranger answered, without raising His eyes from the ground:

'Is it I that have brought you here? Then it is well.'

There was a titter—a woman's giggle rising above the rest. The Stranger, raising His head, looked towards where the speaker stood.

'It were well if most of you should die to-night. O people of no understanding, that discern the little things and cannot see the greater, that have made gods of your bellies, and but minister unto your bodies, what profiteth it whether you live or whether you die? Neither in heaven nor on earth is there a place for you. What, then, is it that you do here?'

A man replied:

'It seems that you are someone in particular. We want to know who you are, according to your own statement.'

'I am He on whose name, throughout the whole of this great city, men call morning, noon, and night. And yet you do not know Me. No! neither do those know Me that call upon Me most.'

'Ever heard of Hanwell?' asked one. 'Perhaps there's some that have known you there.'

The questioner was called to order.

'Stow that! Let's know what he's got to say! Let's hear him out!'

The original inquirer continued.

'For what have you come here?'

'For what?' The Stranger looked up towards the skies. 'It is well that you should ask. I am as one who has lost his way in a strange land, among a strange people; yet it was to Mine own I came, in Mine own country.'

There was an interval of silence. When the inquirer spoke again, it was in less aggressive tones.

'Sir, there is a music in your voice which seems to go to my heart.'

'Friend!' The Stranger stretched out His hand towards the speaker. 'Friend! Would that it would go to all your hearts, the music that is in Mine—that the sound of it would go forth to all the world! It was for that I came.'

This time there was none that answered. It was as though there was that in the Stranger's words which troubled His listeners—which made them uneasy. Here and there one began to steal away. Presently, as the silence continued, the number of these increased. Among them was the inquirer; the Stranger spoke to him as he turned to go.

'It was but seeming—the music which seemed to speak to your heart?'

Although the words were quietly uttered, they conveyed a sting; the man to whom they were addressed was plainly disconcerted.

'Sir, I cannot stay here all night. I am a married man; I must go home.'

'Go home.'

'Besides, the gates will soon be shut, and late hours don't agree with me; I have to go early to business.'

'Go home.'

'But, at the same time, if you wish me to stop with you—'

'Go home.'

The man slunk away, as if ashamed; the Stranger followed him with His eyes. When he had gone a few yards he hesitated, stopped, turned, and, when he saw that the Stranger's eyes were fixed on him, he made as if to retrace his steps. But the Stranger said:

'Go home.'

Taking the gently spoken words as a positive command, the man, as if actuated by an uncontrollable impulse, or by sudden fear, wheeling round again upon his heels, ran out of the park as fast as he was able. When the man had vanished, the Stranger, looking about Him, found that the number of His attendants had dwindled to a scanty few. To them He said:

'Why do you stay? Why do you, also, not go home?'

A fellow replied—his coat was buttoned to his chin; his hands were in his pockets; a handkerchief was round his neck:

'Well, gov'nor, I reckon it's because some of us ain't got much of a 'ome to go to. I know I ain't. A seat in 'ere'll be about my mark—that is, if the coppers'll let me be.'

Again the Stranger's glance passed round the remnant which remained. As the fellow's speech suggested, it was a motley gathering. All told, it numbered, perhaps, a dozen—all that was left of the great crowd which had been there a moment ago. Three or four were women, the rest were men. They stood a little distance off, singly—one here and there. As far as could be seen in the uncertain light, all were poorly clad, most were in rags—a tatterdemalion crew, the sweepings of the streets.

'Are you all homeless, as I am?'

A man replied who was standing among those who were farthest off; he spoke as if the question had offended him.

'I ain't 'omeless—no fear! I've got as food a 'ome as anyone need want to 'ave; 'm none o' yer outcasts.'

'Then why do you not go to it?'

'Why? I am a-goin', ain't I? I suppose I can go 'ome when I like, without none o' your interference!'

The man slouched off, grumbling as he went, his hands thrust deep into his trousers pockets, his head sunk between his shoulders. And with him the rest of those who were left went too, some of them sneaking off across the grass, further into the heart of the park, bent nearly double, so as to get as much as possible into the shadow.

The cause of this sudden and general flight was made plain by the approach of a policeman, shouting:

'Now, then! Gates going to be closed! Out you go!'

The Stranger asked of him: 'May I not stay here and sleep upon the grass?

The policeman laughed, as if he thought the question was a joke.

'Not much you mayn't! Grass is damp—might catch cold—take too much care of you for that.'

'Where, then, can I sleep?'

'I don't know where you can sleep. I'm not here to answer questions. You go out!

The Stranger began to do as He was bid. As He was going towards the gate, a man came hastening to His side; he had been holding himself apart, and only now came out of the shadow. He was a little man; his eagerness made him breathless.

'Sir, it's not much of a place we've got, my wife and I, but such as it is, we shall be glad to give You a night's lodging. I can answer for my wife, and the place is clean.'

The Stranger looked at him, and smiled.

'I thank you.'

Together they went out of the park, the new-comer limping, for he was lame of one foot, the Stranger walking at his side. And all those whom they passed stopped, and turned, and looked at them as they went; some of them asking of themselves:

'What is there peculiar about that man?'

For it was as though there had been an unusual quality in the atmosphere as He went by.

Chapter IX

The First Disciple

'This,' said the lame man, 'is where I live. My rooms are on the first floor. My name is Henry Fenning. I am a shoemaker. My wife helps me at my trade. Our son lives with us, he's a little chap, just nine, and, like me, he's lame.'

The man had conducted the Stranger to a street opening on to the Brompton Road. Even in that uncertain light it could be seen that the houses stood in need of repairs; they were of irregular construction, small, untidy, old. On the ground floor of the one in which he had paused was a shop, a little one; the shop front was four shutters wide. One surmised, from the pictures on the wall, that it sold sweetstuff and odds and ends. The man's manner was anxious, timid, as if, while desirous that his Visitor should take advantage of such hospitality as he could offer, he yet wished to inform Him as to the kind of place He might expect. The Stranger smiled; there was that in His smile which seemed to fill His companion with a singular sense of elation.

'It is good of you to give Me what you can.'

The shoemaker laughed gently, as if his laughter was inspired by a sudden consciousness of gladness.

'It is good of You to take what I can give.' He opened the door. 'Wait a moment while I show You a light.' Striking a match, he held it above his head. 'Take care how You come in; the boards are rough.' The Stranger, entering, followed His host up the narrow stairs, into a room on the first floor. 'Mary, I have brought you a Visitor.'

At the utterance of the name the Stranger started.

'Mary!' He exclaimed. 'Blessed are you among women!'

It was a small apartment—work-room, living-room, kitchen, all in one. Implements of the shoemaker's trade were here and there; some partly finished boots were on a bench at one side. The man's wife was seated at a sewing-machine, working; she rose, as her husband entered, to give him greeting. She was a rosy-faced woman, of medium height, but broadly built, with big brown eyes, about forty years of age. She observed the Stranger with wondering looks.

'Sir, I seem to know You.'

And the Stranger said:

'I know you.'

The woman turned to her husband.

'Who is this?'

Her husband replied:

'It is the Welcome Guest. Give Him to eat and to drink, and after, He would sleep.'

The woman put some cold meat and cheese and bread upon a small table, which she drew into the centre of the floor.

'Sir, this is all I have.'

'I know it.' He took the chair which her husband offered. 'Come and sit and eat and drink with Me.'

The man and his wife sat with Him at the table, and they ate and drank together. When the meal was finished, He said:

'You are the first that have given Me food. What you have given Me shall be given you, and more.'

Presently the shoemaker came to the Stranger.

'Sir, in our bedroom we have only one bed. If You will sleep in it, my wife will make up another for us here upon the floor. We shall do very well.'

In the bedroom the Stranger saw that a child slept in a little bed which was against a wall. The shoemaker explained.

'It is my son. He will not trouble You. He sleeps very sound.'

The Stranger bent over the bed.

'In his sleep he smiles.'

'Yes, he often does. He has happy dreams. And he comes of a smiling stock.'

The Stranger turned to the lame man.

'Do you often smile?'

'Yes; why not? God has been very good to me.'

'God is good to all alike.'

'That's what my wife and I say to each other; but it's only the lucky ones who know it.'

When the shoemaker and his wife were alone in the living-room together, they kissed and gave thanks unto God. For they said:

'This night the Lord is with us. Blessed is the name of the Lord!'

In the morning, when it was full day, the boy woke up and went to the bed on which the Stranger lay asleep, crying:

'Father!'

And the Stranger was roused, and saw the boy standing at his side. He stretched out His arms to him.

'My son!'

But the boy shrank back.

'You are not my father. Where is my father and my mother?'

'They are in the next room, asleep. They have given Me their bed. And, because they have done so, I am your Father too. So in your sleep you smiled?'

'Did I? I expect it was because I dreamed that I was happy.'

'Was your happiness but a dream?'

'While I was asleep. Now I am awake I know I'm happy.'

'But you are lame?'

'So's father. I don't mind being lame if father is.'

The Stranger was still. He smiled, and touched the child upon the shoulder. And the boy gave a sudden cry. He drew up his night-shirt, and looked down at his right leg.

'Why, it's straight!—like the other.' He began to move about the room. 'I'm not lame! I'm not lame!' All aglow with excitement, he went running through the door. 'Father! mother! my leg's gone straight! I can run about like other boys. Look!—I'm no longer lame!'

When his mother saw that it was so, she took him into her arms and cried:

'My boy! my boy! God be thanked for what He has done to you this day!'

When they saw that the Stranger was standing in the doorway the father and mother were silent. Their hearts were too full to find speech easy. But the boy ran to Him.

'Oh, sir! make father's leg straight like mine!'

The Stranger asked of his father:

'Would you have it so?'

But the lame man answered:

'If it may be, let me stay as I am; for if I had not been lame I might never have known Your face.'

To which the Stranger said:

'That is a true saying. For by suffering eyes are opened; so that he who endures most sees best. For to all men God gives gifts.'

The woman busied herself in making breakfast ready. When they were at table, the lame man said:

'Lord, if You will not stay with us, may we come with You?'

'Nay; you are with Me although you stay. For where My own are, I am.'

'Lord, suffer me to come! Suffer it, Lord!'

'If you will, come, until you find the way too long and the path too hard for your feet to travel; for the road by which I go is not an easy one.' He turned to the woman. 'Do you come also?'

'If You will, I will stay at home, to make ready against You come again.'

He answered:

'You have not chosen the worse part.'

While they had been sitting at breakfast the boy had run out into the street, and told first to one and then to another how, with a touch, a wonderful Stranger had straightened his leg, so that he was no longer lame. And, since they could see for themselves that he was healed of his lameness, the tale was quickly noised about; so that when the Stranger came out of the shoemaker's house, He found that a number of people awaited Him without. A woman came pushing through the crowd, bearing a crooked child in her arms.

'Heal my son also! Make him straight like the other!'

And being moved by pity for the child, He touched him, so that he sprang from his mother's arms, and stood before them whole. And all the people were amazed, saying:

'What manner of man is this, that makes the lame to walk with a touch?'

So when He came out into the Brompton Road He was already attended by a crowd, some crying:

'This is the man who works miracles!'

Others:

'Bring out your sick!'

With each step He took the crowd increased, so that when He came to the narrow part of Knightsbridge the street became choked and the traffic blocked. The people, because there were so many, pressed against Him so that He could not move, and there began to be danger of a riot.

The lame man, who found it difficult to keep close to His side, said to Him:

'Lord, if You do not send them from us we shall be hurt.'

But He replied:

'It is to these I have come, although they know it not. If I send them from us, why did I come?'

When they reached that portion of the road where it grows wider in front of the park, the pressure became less. But still the crowd increased.

'He goes to the hospital,' they cry, 'to heal the sick with a touch.'

And some ran on to St. George's Hospital, and pushed past the porters up the stairs and into the wards, and began to lift the sick out of their beds. And those who could walk, being persuaded by them that had run on, went out into the streets. So that when He came, He found awaiting Him a strange collection of the sick, who were ill of all manner of diseases. And the people cried:

'Heal them!—heal them with a touch!'

But He replied:

'What is it you ask of Me? I came not to heal the sick, but to call sinners to repentance.'

They cried the more:

'Heal them!—heal them with a touch!'

'If I heal them, what then? Of what shall they be healed? Of what avail to heal the body if the spirit continues sick?'

But they persisted in their exclamations. While still they pressed on Him, an inspector of police edged his way through the crowd.

'I don't know who you are, sir, but you are doing a very dangerous thing in causing these people to behave like this.'

'Suffer Me first to do as they ask.'

He stretched out His hand and touched those that were sick, so that they were whole. But when they came to look for Him who had done them this service, behold He was gone. And the lame man had gone with Him.

Chapter X

The Deputation

He came, with His disciple to a gate which led into a field, through which there ran a stream. It was high noon. He entered the gate, and sat beside the stream. And the lame man sat near by. The Stranger watched the water as it plashed over the stones on its race to the mill. When presently He sighed, the lame man said:

'I have money; there is a village close handy. Let me go and buy food, and bring it to you here.'

But He answered:

'We shall not want for food. There is one who comes to offer it to us now.'

Even as He spoke a carriage drew up in the road on the other side of the hedge. A lady, standing up in it, looked through a pair of glasses into the field. Bidding the footman open the carriage-door, alighting, she came through the gate to where He sat with His disciple beside the stream. She was a woman of about forty years of age, very richly dressed. As she walked, with her skirts held well away from the grass, she continued to stare through the glasses, which were attached to a long gold handle. Looking from one to the other, her glance rested, on the Stranger.

I Are you the person of whom such extraordinary stories are being told? You look it—you must be—you are. George Horley just told me he saw you on the Shaldon Road. I don't know how he knew it was you—and his manner was most extraordinary—but he's a sharp fellow, and I shouldn't be surprised if he was right. Tell me, are you that person?'

'I am He that you know not of.'

'My dear sir, that doesn't matter one iota. What I've heard of you is sufficient introduction for me. I don't know if you're aware that this field is mine, and that you're trespassing. I'm very particular about not allowing the villagers to come in here—they will go after the mushrooms. But if you'll take a seat in my carriage I shall be very happy to put you up for a day or two. I'm Mrs. Montara, of Weir Park. I have some very delightful people staying with me, who will be of the greatest service to you in what I understand is your propaganda. Most interesting what I've heard of you, I'm sure.' The Stranger was silent. 'Well, will you come?'

'Woman, return to your own place. Leave Me in peace.'

'I don't admire your manners, my good man, especially after my going out of my way to be civil to you. Is that all the answer you have to give?'

'What have I to do with you, or you with Me? I am not that new thing which you seek. I am of old.'

He looked at her. The great lady shrank back a little, as if abashed.

'Whoever you are, I shall be glad to have you as my guest.'

'I am not found in rich women's houses. They are too poor. They offer nothing. They seek only to obtain.'

'I offer you, in the way of hospitality, whatever you may want.'

'You cannot offer Me the one thing which I desire.'

'What is that?'

'That you should know Me even as you are known. For unless you know Me I have nothing, and less than nothing, and there is nothing in the world that is at all to be desired. For if I have come unto Mine own, and they know Me not, then My coming indeed is vain. Go! Strip yourself and your house, and be ashamed. In the hour of your shame come to Me again.'

'If that's the way you talk to me, get up and leave my field, before I have you locked up for trespass.'

He stood up, and said to the lame man:

'Come!'

And they went out of the field, and passed through that place without staying to eat or drink. In the next village an old woman, who was standing at a cottage gate, stopped them as they were passing on.

'You are tired. Come in and rest.'

And they entered into her house. And she gave them food, refusing the money which the lame man offered.

'I have a spare bedroom. You can have it if you'd like to stay the night, and you'll be kindly welcome.'

So they stayed with her that night.

And in the morning, while it was yet early, they arose and went upon their way. And when they had gone some distance they heard on the road behind them the sound of a horse's hoofs. And when they turned, they saw that a wagonette was being driven hotly towards them. When, on reaching them, it stopped, they saw that it contained five men. One, leaning over the side, said to the Stranger:

'Are you he we are looking for?' The Stranger replied:

'I am He whom you seek.'

'That is,' added a second man, 'you are the individual who is stated to have been performing miracles in London?'

The Stranger only said:

'I am He whom you seek.'

'In that case,' declared the first speaker, 'we are very fortunate.'

He scrambled out on to the road, a short, burly man, with restless bright eyes and an iron-gray beard. He wore a soft, round, black felt hat, and was untidily dressed. He seemed to be in perpetual movement, in striking contrast to the Stranger's immutable calm.

'Will you come with us in the wagonette?' he demanded. 'Or shall we say what we have to say to you here? It is early; we're in the heart of the country; no one seems about. If we cross the stile which seems to lead into that little copse, we could have no better audience-chamber, and need fear no interruption.'

'Say what you have to say to Me here.'

'Good! Then, to begin with, we'll introduce ourselves.'

His four companions were following each other out of the wagonette. As they descended he introduced each one in turn.

'This is Professor Wilcox Wilson, the pathologist. Professor Wilson does not, however, confine himself to one subject, but is interested in all live questions of the day; and, while he keeps an open mind, seeks to probe into the why and wherefore of all varieties of phenomena. This is the Rev. Martin Philipps, the eminent preacher and divine, who joins to a liberal theology a far-reaching interest in the cause of suffering humanity. Augustus Jebb, perhaps the greatest living authority on questions of social science and the welfare of the wage-earning classes. John Anthony Gibbs, who may be said to represent the religious conscience of England in the present House of Commons. I myself am Walter S. Treadman, journalist, student, preacher, and, I hope, humanitarian. I only know that where there is a cry of pain, there my heart is. I heard that you were in this neighbourhood, and lost no time in requesting these gentlemen to associate themselves with me in the appeal which I am about to make to you. Therefore I beg of you to regard me as, in a sense, a deputation from England. Your answer will be given to England. And on that account, if no other, we implore you to weigh, with the utmost care, any words which you may utter. To come to the point: Do we understand you to assert that the feats with which you have set all London agape are, in the exact sense of the word, miraculous—that is, incapable of a natural interpretation?'

'Why do you speak such words to Me?'

'For an obvious reason. England is at heart religious. Though, for the moment, she may seem torpid, it needs but a breath to fan the smouldering embers into a mighty blaze which will light the world, and herald in the brightness of the eternal dawn. If these things which you have done are of God, then you must be of Him, and from Him, and may be the bearer of a message to the myriads whose ears are strained to listen. Therefore I implore you to answer.'

'What I have done, I have done not as a sign, nor to be magnified in the eyes of men, but to dry the tears which were in their eyes.'

'Then they were miracles. So the question at once assumes another phase—Who are you?'

'I am He whom you know not of, though you call often on My name.'

'You are the Christ—the Lord Christ?'

Professor Wilson laid his hand on Mr. Treadman's arm.

'You go too fast. No such assertion has been made; no such claim has been put forth. I may add that there has been no such outrage on good taste.'

The Rev. Martin Philipps interposed.

'Good taste is not necessarily outraged by such a claim; or, if it is now, it was also at the first. Jesus was a man, such as we are, such as this one here.'

Mr. Jebb agreed.

'And a labouring man at that. He worked with His own hands—a wage-earner if ever there was one.'

'But,' pleaded the Professor, 'at least something was known of His pedigree, of His credentials.'

'I am not so sure of that.'

'Nor I.'

'At any rate, let us proceed as if we were reasonable beings, and actuated by the dictates of common-sense. Permit me to put one or two questions: Are you an Englishman?'

'I am of a country which also you know not of. Thither I return to meet Mine own.'

'Your answer is evasive. Allow me to point out, with the greatest possible deference, that it is on record how Jesus originally damaged His own case by the vagueness of the replies which He gave to questions and the want of lucidity which characterised His description of Himself. If you claim any, even the remotest, connection with Him, let me advise you to avoid His errors.'

'You know not what you say, you fool of wisdom!'

'Lord,' cried Mr. Treadman,' I believe—help Thou my unbelief! I believe because faith is the great want of the age, and it shall remove mountains; I believe because belief is like the pinch of yeast which, being dropped into the dough, leavens the whole. The leaven spreads through the whole body politic, so that out of a little thing proceeds a great. And, Lord, suffer Thy servant to entreat with Thee. Lose no time. Thy people wait—have waited long; they cry aloud; they look always for the little speck upon the sky; they lift up their hands and beat against heaven's gates. Speak but the word—the one word which Thou canst speak so easily! A whole world will leap into Thy arms.'

'Their will, not mine, be done?'

'Nay, Lord, not so—not so! Esteem me not guilty of such presumption; but I have lived among them, and have seen how the world labours and is in pain, and how Thy people are crushed beneath heavy burdens which press them down almost to the confines of the pit. And therefore out of the fulness and anguish of my knowledge I cry: Lord, come quickly—come quickly! Lose not a moment's time!'

'Your knowledge is greater than Mine?'

'Nay, Lord, I do not say that, nor think it. But Thou art immortal; Thy children are mortal—very mortal. I understand the agony of longing with which they look for Your presence—Your very presence—in their midst.'

'They that know Me know that I am ever with them. They that do not know Me know not that they see Me before their eyes.'

'You speak in a spiritual sense, I in a material. I know with what a passionate yearning they desire to see you with their mortal eyes, flesh of their flesh, bone of their bone—a man like unto themselves.'

'You also seek a sign?'

'Who does not seek a sign? The soldier watches for the sign which shows that his general is in command; the child looks for the sign which proclaims his parent is at hand; the explorer searches for the sign which shows his guide is leading him aright. There is chaos where there is no sign.'

'Did I not say I am He you know not of? Those who know Me need no sign.'

'Nor, in that sense, do I need one either. I have been unfortunate in my choice of words if I have conveyed the impression that I do.'

'I have suffered you too much.' He turned to the lame man. 'Come!'

The Stranger and His disciple were continuing on their way when Mr. Treadman's companions placed themselves in the path.

'Mr. Treadman's well-known command of language,' explained the Professor, 'is likely to obscure the purpose of our presence here. We have come to ask you to accompany us to town as our guest, and to avail yourself of our services in placing, in the most efficient and practical manner possible, your views and wishes before the country as a whole.'

'In other words,' observed the Rev. Martin Philipps, 'we are here as the Lord's servants, desirous to do His work and His will.'

'Having at heart,' continued Mr. Jebb, 'the welfare—spiritual, moral, and physical—of the struggling millions.'

'Acting also,' added Mr. Gibbs, 'as the mouthpiece of Christ's kingdom as it exists in our native land.'

The Professor's tone, as he commented on his colleagues' remarks, was a little grim.

'What my friends say is, no doubt, very excellent in its way; but the main point still is—Will you come with us? If so, here is a conveyance. You have only to jump in at once, and we shall be in time to catch a fast train back to town. My strong advice to you is, Be practical, and come.'

'Suffer Me to go My way.'

'Is that your answer? Remember that history records how, on a previous occasion, a great opportunity was frittered away for lack of a little business acumen. There can be no doubt that the great need of the hour is a practical religion. It is quite within the range of possibility that you might go far towards placing such a propaganda on a solid basis. Consider, therefore; before you treat our offer with contempt.'

He made no answer, but went along the road, with the lame man at His side.

For some seconds the deputation stood staring after Him. Then the Professor gave expression to his feelings in these words:

'An impracticable person.'

The Rev. Martin Philipps had something to say on this curt summing up of the position.

'I think, Professor, that what you call practicality is likely to be your stumbling-block. In your sense, God is not always practical.'

'In a country of practical men that is unfortunate.'

'When you say practical you mean material. There is something higher than materiality.'

'The material and the spiritual, Philipps, are more closely allied than you may suppose. It is useless to ask a mere man to give primary attention to his spiritual wants when, in a material sense, he lacks everything. To formulate such a demand, even by inference, is to play into the hands of the plutocracy.'

'Still,' remarked Mr. Gibbs,' I think there might have been more said of the things of the soul, and less of the things of the body. It is the soul of England we are here to plead for, not its mere corporeal husk.'

While they talked Mr. Treadman stood looking after the retreating Stranger. Suddenly he started running, calling as he went:

'Lord, Lord, suffer that I may come with You!'

He went on, with the lame man at His side, and Mr. Treadman at His heels, calling persistently: 'Suffer that I may come with You!' until presently He turned, saying:

'Why do you continue to entreat that I should suffer you? Have I forbidden you to come?'

For a time Mr. Treadman was still. But continually he broke again into speech, talking of this thing and of that.

But there was none that answered him.

Chapter XI

The Second Disciple

They lay that night at the house of a certain curate, who stopped the Stranger, saying:

'You are he of whom I have heard?'

Mr. Treadman said:

'It is the Lord—the Lord Christ! He has come again!'

The Stranger rebuked Mr. Treadman.

'Peace! Why do you trouble Me with your babbling tongue?' To the curate He said: 'What do you want of Me?'

'Nothing but to offer you shelter for the night. I cannot give you much, for I am poor, and have a small house and a large family, but such as I have is at your service. Not that I wish you to understand that my action marks my approval of your proceedings, of which, as I say, I have heard. For I am an ordained priest of the Church of England, and have sufficient trouble with dissent and such-like fads already. But I am a Christian, and, I trust, a gentleman, and in that dual capacity would not wish one of whom I have heard such remarkable things to remain in need of shelter when near my house.'

So they went with the curate. But the family was found to be so large, and the house so small, that there was not room within its walls for three unexpected guests. So it was arranged that they would sleep in the loft over the stable where hay was kept. Thither, after supper, the Stranger and the lame man repaired. But Mr. Treadman remained talking to the host.

They stood outside the house in the moonlight, looking towards the loft in which the Stranger sought slumber.

'That is a good man,' said the curate, 'and a strange one. He has filled my mind with curious thoughts.'

'It is the Lord! said Mr. Treadman.

'The Lord?' The curate regarded the speaker with a peculiar smile. 'Are you mad, sir? Or do you think I am?'

'It is the Lord!' Mr. Treadman held out his clenched fists in front of him, as if to add weight to his assertion. 'I know it of a surety!'

'Does it not occur to you what an awful thing it would be if what you say were true?' Awful? How awful?'

'When He came before He found them unprepared—so unprepared that they could not believe it was He. What would it not mean if, at His Second Coming, He found us still unready? He might be moving among us, and we not know it; we might meet Him in the street, and pass Him by. The human mind is not at its best when it is wholly unprepared: it cannot twist itself hither and thither without even a moment's notice. And our civilisation is so complex that the first result of an unexpected Advent would be to plunge it into chaos. Saints and sinners alike would be thrown off their balance. There would be a carnival of confusion. The tragedy which rings down the ages might be reenacted. Christ might be crucified again by Christian hands.'

'We must avoid it! We must avoid it! We must prepare the people's minds; we must let them know that His reign is about to begin. They need but the knowledge to fill the world with songs of gladness.'

'You really believe your friend is a supernatural being?'

'It is the Lord! I know it of a surety! You call yourself His minister. Is it possible you do not know Him, too?'

'No; I do not. For one thing, I do not think that, really and truly, I have ever contemplated the possibility of such an occurrence. To me the Second Coming has been an abstraction—a nebulous something that would not happen in my time. Yet he troubles me, the more so since I remember that good men must have stood in His presence aforetime, and yet not have known Him for what He was, although He troubled them. However, it may be written to the good of my account that for your friend I have done what I could.'

The curate returned into his house. But it was long before Mr. Treadman sought the shelter of the loft. He passed here and there in an agony of mind which grew greater as the night went on. By the light of the waning moon he wrought himself into a frenzy of supplication.

'O Lord, I say it in no spirit of irreverence, but in a sense, You do not understand the idiosyncrasies and character of those to whom You are about to appeal. To come to them unheralded, to move about among them unannounced, will be useless—ah, and worse than useless! O Lord, do not take them by surprise. Sound, at least, one trumpet blast. Come to them as You should come—as their Christ and King. It needs such a very little, and You will have them at Your feet. Do not lose all for want of such a little. Let me tell them You are on the way, that You are here, that You are in their very midst. Let me be John Baptist. I promise You that I shall not be a voice crying in the wilderness, but that at the proclamation of the tidings, trumpeted by all the presses of the land, and from ten thousand pulpits, from all the cities and the villages will issue happy, hot-footed crowds, eager to look upon the face they have had pictured in their hearts their whole lives long, and on the form they have yearned to see, filled with but one desire—to lay themselves at the feet of their Christ and King! But, Lord, if no one tells them You are here, how shall they know it? They are but foolish folk, fashioned as Thou knowest they are fashioned. If You come upon them at the market or the meeting, and take them unawares, they will not know that it is You. Suffer me first to spread the glad tidings through all the land. I have but to put a plain statement on the wires, and foot it with my name, and there is not a newspaper in an English-speaking country which will not give it a prominent place in its morning's issue. Suffer me at least to do so much as that.'

The figure of the Stranger appeared at the door which led into the loft; and He spoke to Mr. Treadman, saying:

'You know not what are the things of which you speak, as is the manner of men. Are you, then, so ignorant as not to be aware that God's ways are not as men's? Let your soul cease from troubling. God asks not to learn of you. He made you; He holds you in the hollow of His hand; you are the dust of the balance. Come, and sleep.'

Mr. Treadman went up into the loft, crying like a child. Almost as soon as he laid himself down among the sweetness of the hay his tears were dried, and his eyes were closed in slumber. And he and the lame man slept together.

But the Stranger sought not sleep. Through the night He did not close His eyes. As the day came near He stood looking down upon the sleepers. And His face was sorrowful.

'Men are but little children: if they had but the heart of a child!'

And He went down the loft out into the morning.

And presently the lame man woke up and found that he was alone with Mr. Treadman. So he began to scramble down the ladder. As he went, because of his haste and his lameness, he stumbled and fell. The noise of his fall woke Mr. Treadman, who hurried down the ladder also. At the foot he found the lame man, who was rising to his feet.

'Are you hurt?' he asked.

'I think not. I am only shaken. The Lord has gone!'

'Gone! Lean on me. We will find Him.'

The two went out into the lifting shadows, the lame man on Mr. Treadman's arm. The country was covered by a morning mist. It was damp and cold. The light was puzzling. Mr. Treadman looked to the right and left.

'Which way can He have gone?'

'There! there He is! I see Him on the road. My leg is better; let us hasten. We shall catch Him.'

'No. Do not let us catch Him. Let us follow and see which way He goes. I have a reason.'

'But He will know you are following, and your reason.'

'May be. Still let us follow.'

Mr. Treadman had his way. They followed at a distance. As was his habit, Mr. Treadman talked as he went.

'It is strange that He should try to leave us like this, when He knows that we would leave no stone unturned to follow Him, through life, to death.'

'It is not strange. He does nothing strange.'

'You think not?'

'How can the Lord of all the earth do wrong?'

'There is something in that.' Mr. Treadman was still for a time. 'Yet He runs a great risk of wrecking His entire cause.' The lame man said nothing. 'It is necessary that the people should be told that He is coming, that their minds should be prepared. If they have authentic information of His near neighbourhood, then He will triumph at once and for always. If not—if He comes on them informally, unheralded, unannounced, then there will be a frightful peril of His cause being again dragged in the mire.'

Yet the lame man said nothing. But Mr. Treadman continued to talk, apparently careless of the fact that he had the conversation to himself.

When they came to a place where there were cross-roads, and Mr. Treadman saw which way He went, he caught the lame man by the arm.

'I thought as much! He's heading for London.'

Taking out a note-book, he began to write in it with a fountain pen, still continuing to walk and to talk.

'I know this country well. There's a telegraph-office about a mile along the road. It ought to be open by the time we get there. If it isn't, I'll rouse them up. I'll send word to some friends of mine—men and women whose lifelong watchword has been God and His gospel—that He is coming. They will run to meet Him. They will bring with them some of the brightest spirits now living; and He will have a foretaste of that triumph which, if matters are properly organised, awaits Him. He shall enter on His inheritance as the Christ and King, and pain, sin, sorrow, shall cease throughout the world, if He will but suffer me to make clear the way. Tell me, my friend,—you don't appear to be a loquacious soul,—don't you think that to be prepared is half the battle?'

But the lame man made no reply. He only kept his eyes fixed on the Figure which went in front.

His companion's irresponsive mood did not appear to trouble Mr. Treadman. He never ceased to talk and write, except when he broke into the words of a hymn, which he sung in a loud, clear voice, as if he wished that all the country-side should hear.

'There,' he cried, after they had gone some distance, 'is the place I told you of. The village is just round the bend in the road. If I remember rightly, the post-office is on the left as you enter. Soon the telegraph shall be on the side of the Lord, and the glad tidings be flashing up to town. We're not twenty miles from London. Within an hour a reception committee should be on the way. Before noon many longing eyes will have looked with knowledge on the face of the Lord; and joyful hearts shall sing: "Hosanna in the highest! Hallelujah! Christ has come!"'

On their coming to the village Mr. Treadman made haste to the post-office. It was not yet open. He began a violent knocking at the door.

'I must rouse them up. Official hours are as nothing in such a case as this. I must get my messages upon the wires at once, whatever it may cost.'

The lame man made all haste to reach the Stranger that went in front, passing alone through the quiet village street.

PART II

Chapter XII

The Charcoal-burner

When Mr. Treadman had brought the post-office to a consciousness of his presence, and induced the postmaster, with the aid of copious bribes, to do what he desired, some time had passed. On his return into the street neither the Stranger nor the lame man was in sight. At this, however, he was little concerned, making sure of the way they had gone, and of his ability to catch them up. But after he had gone some distance, at the top of his speed, and still saw no sign of the One he sought, he began to be troubled.

'They might have waited. The Lord knew that I was engaged upon His work. Why has He thus left me in the lurch?'

A cart approached. He hailed the driver.

'Have you seen, as you came along, two persons walking along the road towards London?'

'Ay; about half a mile ahead.'

'Half a mile! So much as that! I shall never catch them if I walk. You will have to give me a lift, and make all haste after them.'

He began to bargain with the driver, who, agreeing to his terms, permitted him to climb into his cart, and turning his horse's head, set off after those of whom he had spoken. But they were nowhere to be seen.

'It was here I passed them.'

'Probably they are a little further on. Drive more quickly. We shall see them in a minute. The winding road hides them, and the hedges.'

The driver did as he was bid. But though he went on and on, he saw nothing of those whom he was seeking. Mr. Treadman began to be alarmed.

'It is a most extraordinary thing. Where can He have got to? Is it possible that that lame fellow can have told Him of the message I was sending, and that He has purposely given me the slip? If so, I shall be placed in an embarrassing position. These people are sure to come. Mrs. Powell and Gifford will be off in an instant. They have been looking for the Lord too long not to make all haste to see Him now. For all I know, they may bring half London with them. If they find they have come for nothing, the situation will be awkward. My reputation will be damaged. I ask it with all possible reverence, but why is the Lord so little mindful of His own?'

The driver stopped his horse.

'You must get out here. I must go back. I'll be late as it is.'

'Go back! My man, you must press forward. It is for the Lord that I am looking.'

'The Lord!'

'The Lord Christ. He has come to us again, this time to win the world as a whole, and for ever; and by some frightful accident I have allowed Him to pass out of my sight.'

'I've heard tell of something of the kind. But I don't take no count of such things. There's some as does; but I'm not one. I tell you you must get out. I'm more than late enough already.'

Left stranded in the middle of the road, Mr. Treadman stared after the retreating carter.

'The man has no spiritual side; he's a mere brute! In this age of Christianity and its attendant civilisation, it's wonderful that such creatures should continue to exist. If there are many such, it is a hard task which He has set before Him. He will need all the help which we can give. Why, then, does he seem to slight the efforts of His faithful servant? I don't know what will happen if those people find that they have come from town for nothing. His cause may receive an almost irreparable injury at the very start.'

Those people came. The messages with which he troubled the wires were of a nature to induce them to come. There was Mrs. Miriam Powell, whose domestic unhappiness has not prevented her from doing such good work among fallen women, that it is surprising how their numbers still continue to increase. And there was Harvey Gifford, the founder of that Christian Assistance Society which has done such incalculable service in providing cheap entertainments for the people, and which ceaselessly sends to the chief Continental pleasure resorts hordes of persons, in the form of popular excursions, whose manners and customs are hardly such as are even popularly associated with Christianity. When these two Christian workers received Mr. Treadman's telegram, phrased in the quaint Post–Office fashion— 'Christ is coming to London the Christ I have seen him and am with him and I know he is here walking on the highroad come to him and let your eyes be gladdened meet him if possible between Guildford and Ripley I will endeavour to induce him to come that way about eleven spread the glad tidings so that he enters London as one that comes into his own this is the Lord's doing this is the day of the Lord we triumph all along the line the stories told of his miracles are altogether inadequate state that positively to all inquirers as from me no more can be said within the limits of a telegram for your soul's sake fail not to be on the Ripley road in time the faithful servant of the Lord—Treadman'—their minds were made up on the instant. London was ringing with inchoate rumours. Scarcely within living memory had the public mind been in a state of more curious agitation. The truth or falsehood of the various statements which were made was the subject of general controversy. Where two or three were gathered together, there was discussed the topic of the hour. It seemed, from Treadman's telegram, that he of whom the tales were told was coming back in town, which he had quitted in such mysterious fashion. It seemed that Treadman himself actually believed he was the Christ.

Could two such single-minded souls, in the face of such a message, delay from making all haste in the direction of the Ripley road?

Yet before they went, and as they went, they did their best to spread the tidings. Mr. Treadman had done his best to spread them too. He had sent messages to heads of the Salvation and Church Armies, and of the various great religious societies, to ministers of all degrees and denominations, and, indeed, to everyone of whom, in his haste, he could think as being, in a religious or philanthropic, or, in short, in any sense, in that curious place—the public eye.

And presently various specimens of these persons were on their way to the Ripley road—some journeying by train, some on foot, some on horseback; a large number, both men and women, upon bicycles, and others in as heterogeneous a collection of vehicles as one might wish to see. Sundry battalions of the Salvation Army confided themselves to vans such as are used for beanfeasts and Sunday–School treats. They shouted hymns; their bands made music by the way.

He whom all these people were coming out to see had gone with the lame man across a field-path to a little wood, which lay not far from the road. In the centre of the wood they found a clearing, where the charcoal-burners had built their huts and plied their trade. An old man watched the smouldering heap. He sat on some billets of wood, one of which he was carving with a clumsy knife. The Stranger found a seat upon another heap, and the lame man placed himself, cobbler fashion, upon the turf at His side. For some moments nothing was said. Then the old man broke the silence.

'Strangers hereabouts?'

He replied:

'My abiding-place is not here.'

'So I thought. I fancied I hadn't seen you round about these parts; yet there's something about you I seem to know. Come in here to rest?'

'It is good to rest.'

'That's so; there's nothing like it when you're tired. You look as if you was tired, and you look as if you'd known trouble. There's a comfortable look upon your face which never comes upon a man or woman's face unless they have known trouble. I always says that no one's any good until it shines out of their eyes.'

'Sorrow and joy walk hand in hand.'

'That's it: they walk hand in hand, and you never know one till you've known the other, just as you never know what health is till you've had to go without it. Do you see what I'm doing here? I'm a charcoal-burner by trade, but by rights I ought to have been a wood-carver. There's few men can do more with a knife and a bit of wood than I can. All them as knows me knows it. That's a cross I'm carving. My daughter's turned religious, and she's a fancy that I should cut her a cross to hang in her room, so that, as she says, she can always think of Christ crucified. To me that's a queer start. I always think of Him as Christ crowned.'

'He is crowned.'

'Of course He is. As I put it, what He done earned Him the V.C. It's with that cross upon His breast I like to think of Him. In what He done I can't see what people see to groan about. It was something to glory in, to be proud of.'

'He was crucified by those to whom He came.'

'There is that. They must have been a silly lot, them Jews. They didn't know what they was doing of.'

'Which man knows what he does, or will let God know, either?'

'It's a sure and certain thing that some of us ain't over and above wise. There do be a good many fools about. I mind that I said to my daughter a good score times: "Don't you have that Jim Bates." But she would. Now he's took himself off and she's took to religion. It's a true fact she didn't know what she was doing of when she had him.'

'Did Jim Bates know what he was doing?'

'I shouldn't be surprised but what he didn't. He never did know much, did Jim. It isn't everyone as can live with my daughter, as he had ought to have known. She's kept house for me these twelve year, so I do know. She always were a contrary piece, she were.'

'The world is full of discords, but He who plays upon it tunes one note after another. In the end it will be all in tune.'

'There's a good many of us as'll wish that we was deaf before that time comes.'

'Because many men are deaf they take no heed of the harmonies.'

'There's something in that. I shouldn't wonder but what there's a lot of music as no one notices. The more you speak, the more I seem to know you. You're like a voice I've heard talking to me when the speaker was hid by the darkness.'

'I have spoken to you often.'

'Ay, I believe you have. I thought I knew you from the first. I felt so comfortable when you came. All the morning I've been troubled, what with worries at home and the pains what seems all over me, so that I can't move about as I did use to; and then when I saw you coming along the path all the trouble was at an end.'

'I heard you calling as I passed along the road.'

'You heard me calling? Why, I never opened my mouth!'

'Not the words of the lips are heard in heaven, but none ever called from his heart in vain.'

The charcoal-burner rose from his heap of billets.

'Why, who are you?' He came closer, peering with his dim eyes. 'It is the Lord! What an old fool I am not to have known You from the first! Yet I felt that it was You.'

'You know Me, although you knew Me not.'

'And me that's known You all my life, and my old woman what knew You too! Anyhow, I'd have seen You before long.'

'You have seen Me from the first.'

'Not plain—not plain. I've heard You, and I've known that You was there, but I haven't seen You as I've tried to. You know the sort of chap I am—a silly old fool what's been burning since I was a little nipper. I ain't no scholar. The likes of me didn't have no schooling when I was young, and I ain't no hand at words; but You know how I'm all of a twitter, and there ain't no words what will tell how glad I am to see You. Like the silly old jackass that I am, I'm a-cryin'!'

The Stranger stood up, holding out His hand.

'Friend!'

The charcoal-burner put his gnarled, knotted, and now trembling hand into the Stranger's palm.

'Lord! Lord!'

'So often I have heard you call upon My Name.'

'Ay, in the morning when the day was young; at noon, when the work was heavy; at night, when rest had come. Youth and man, You've been with me all the time, and with my old woman, too.'

'She and I met long since.'

'My old woman! She was a good one to me, she was.'

'And to Me.'

'A better wife no man could have. It weren't all lavender, her life wasn't, but it smelt just as sweet as if it were.'

'The perfume of it ascended into heaven.'

'My temper, it be short. There were days when I was sharp with her. She'd wait till it was over, and me ashamed, and then she'd say: "Each time, William, you be in a passion it do bring you nearer to the Lord." I'd ask her how she made that out, and she'd say: "'Tis like a bit of 'lastic, William. When you pulls it the ends get drawed apart, but when you lets it go again, the ends come closer than they was before. When you be in a passion, William, you draws yourself away from the Lord's end; when your passion be over, back you goes with a rush, until you meets Him plump. Only," she'd say, "don't you draw away too often, lest the 'lastic break." I never could tell if she were laughing at me, or if she weren't. But I do know she did make me feel terrible ashamed. I used to wonder if the Lord's temper ever did go short.'

'The Lord is like unto men—He knows both grief and anger.'

'Seems to me as how He wouldn't be the Lord if He didn't. He feels what we feels, or how'd He be able to help us?'

'The Lord and His children are of one family. Did you not know that?'

'I knowed it. But there's them as thinks the Lord's a fine gentleman, what's always a-looking you up and down, and that you ain't never to come near Him without your best clothes and your company manners on. Seems to me the Lord don't only want to know you now and then, He wants to know you right along. If you can't go to Him because you be mucked with charcoal, it be bitter hard.'

'You know you can.'

'I do know you can, I do. When I've been as black as black can be I've felt Him just as close as in the chapel Sundays.'

'The Lord is not here or there, in the house or in the field; He is with His children.'

'Hebe that! He be!'.

Chapter XIII

A Triumphal Entry

The people came to meet the Lord upon the Ripley road, and they were not a few.

The first that found Mr. Treadman were Mrs. Powell and Harvey Gifford. They took a fly from the station, bidding the driver drive straight on. Nor had they gone far before they came on Mr. Treadman sitting on a gate. They cried to him:

'What is the meaning of your telegram?'

'It means that the Lord has come again, in very surety and very truth.'

'Are you in earnest?'

'Did they not ask that question of the prophets? Were they in earnest? Then am I.'

'But where is He?'

'He has given me the slip.'

'Given you the slip? What do you mean?'

Mr. Treadman explained. While he did so, others arrived, men and women of all sorts, ranks, and ages. They were agog with curiosity.

'What like is He to look at? Does the sight of Him blind, as it did Moses?'

'Nothing of the sort. He is just an ordinary man, like you and me.'

'An ordinary man! Then how can you tell it is the Lord?'

'He is not to be mistaken. You cannot be in His presence twenty seconds without being sure of it.'

'But—I don't understand! I thought that when He came again it was to be with legions of angels, in pomp and glory, to be the Judge of all the earth.'

'The Jews looked for a material display. They thought He was to come in Majesty. And because, to their unseeing eyes, He appeared as one of themselves, in their disappointment they nailed Him upon a tree. Oh, my friends, don't let a similar mistake be ours! That is the awful, immeasurable peril which already stares us in the face. Because, in His infinite wisdom, for reasons which are beyond our ken, and, perhaps, beyond our comprehension, He has again chosen to put on the guise of our common manhood, let us not, on that account, the less rejoice to see Him, nor let us fail to do Him all possible honour. He has come again unto His children; let His children receive Him with shouts and with Hosannas. It is possible, when He perceives how complete is His dominion over your hearts and minds, that He will be pleased to manifest Himself in that splendour of Godhead for which I know some of you have been confidently looking. Only, until that hour comes, let us not fail to do reverence to the God in man.'

'But where is He? You told us to meet Him on the Ripley road. How can we do Him reverence if we do not know where He is?'

The question came in different forms from many throats. The crowd had grown. The people were eager.

A boy threaded his way among them. He addressed himself to Mr. Treadman.

'Please, sir, there's someone in the wood with Mr. Bates. When I took Mr. Bates his dinner he called him "Lord."'

Presently the crowd were following the boy. He led them some little distance along the road, and then across a field into a wood. There they came upon the Stranger and the charcoal-burner eating together, seated side by side; and the lame man also ate with them, sitting on the ground. Mr. Treadman cried:

'Lord, we have found You again!'

He looked at the people, asking:

'Who are these?'

'They are Your children—Your faithful, loving, eager children, who have come to give You greeting.'

'My children? There are many that call themselves My children that I know not of.'

Mr. Treadman cried:

'Oh, my friends, this is the Lord! Rejoice and give thanks. Many are the days of the years in which you have watched for Him, and waited, and He has come to you at last.'

For the most part the people were still. There were some that pressed forward, but more that hung back. For now that they came near to the Stranger's presence they began to be afraid. Yet Mrs. Powell went close to Him, asking:

'Are you in very deed the Lord?'

He replied:

'Are you of the children of the Lord?

She drew a little back.

'I do not know Him; I do not know Him! Yet I am afraid.'

'Love casteth out fear; but where there is no love, there fear is.'

She drew still more away, saying again:

'I am afraid.'

Mr. Treadman explained:

'We are here to meet You, Lord, and to entreat You to let us come with You to London.'

'Why should you come with Me?'

'Because we are Your children.'

'My children!'

'Yes, Lord, Your children, each in his or her own fashion, but each with his or her whole heart. And because we are Your children, we are here to meet You—many of us at no slight personal inconvenience—to keep You company on the way, so that by our testimony we may begin to make it known that the Lord has come again to be the Judge of all the earth.'

'What know you of the why and wherefore of My coming?'

'Actually nothing. But I am very sure You are here for some great and good purpose, and trust, before long, to prove myself worthy of the Divine confidence. In the meantime I implore You to suffer those who are here assembled to accompany You as a guard of honour, so that You may make, though in a rough-and-ready fashion, a triumphant entry into that great city which is the capital of Your kingdom here on earth.'

'I will come with you.' To the lame man and to the charcoal-burner He said: 'Come also.'

He went with them. And when they came into the road nothing would content Mr. Treadman but that He should get into the fly which had brought Mrs. Powell and Mr. Gifford from the station. The lame man and the charcoal-burner rode with Him. As Mr. Treadman was preparing to mount upon the box Mrs. Powell came.

'What am I to do? I cannot walk all the way. It is too far.'

'Get in also. There is room.'

She shuddered.

'I dare not—I am afraid.'

So the fly went on without her.

As they went the bands played and the people sang hymns. There were some that shouted texts of Scripture and all manner of things. In the towns and villages folk came running out to learn what was the cause of all the hubbub.

'What is it?' they cried.

Mr. Treadman standing up would shout: 'It is the Lord! He has come to us again! Rejoice and give thanks. Come, all ye that are weary and heavy laden, for He has brought you rest.'

They pressed round the fly, so that it could scarcely move.

In a certain place a great man who was driving with his wife, when he saw the crowd and heard what they were saying, was angry, crying with a loud voice:

'What ribaldry is this? What blasphemous words are these you utter? I am ashamed to think that Englishmen should behave in such a fashion.'

Mr. Treadman answered:

'You foolish man! you don't know what it is you say. Yours is the shame, not ours. It is the Lord in very deed!'

The other, still more angry, caused his coachman to place his carriage close beside the fly, intending to reprimand Him whom he supposed to be the cause of the commotion. But when he saw the Stranger he was silent. His wife cried: 'It is the Lord!'

She went quickly from the carriage to the fly. When she reached it she fell on her knees, hiding her face on the seat at the Stranger's side.

'You have my son, my only son!'

He said:

'Be comforted. Your son I know and you I know. To neither of you shall any harm come.'

Her husband called to her.

'Are you mad? What is the meaning of this extraordinary behaviour? Do you wish to cause a public scandal?'

She answered:

'It is the Lord!'

But her husband commanded her:

'Come back into the carriage!'

She cried:

'Lord, let me stay with You. You have my boy; where my boy is I would be also.'

The Stranger said:

'Return unto your husband. You shall stay with Me although you return to him.'

She went back into the carriage weeping bitterly.

The news of the strange procession which was coming went on in front. All the way were people waiting, so that the crowd grew more and more. All that came had to make room for it, waiting till the press was gone. Though the way was long, but few seemed to tire. Those that were at the first continued to the end, the bands playing almost without stopping, and the people singing hymns.

By the time they neared London it was evening. The throng had grown so great the authorities began to be concerned. Policemen lined the roads, ready if necessary to preserve order. But their services were not needed, as Mr. Treadman proclaimed:

'Constables, we are, glad to see you. Representatives of the law, He who comes is the Lord. Therefore shout Hosanna with the best of us and give Him greeting.'

Presently someone pressed a piece of paper into his hand on which was written:

'If the Lord would but stay this night in the house of the chief of sinners.

'MIRIAM POWELL.'

He took a pencil from his pocket, and wrote beneath:

'He shall stay in your house this night, thou daughter of the Lord.

'W. S. T.'

From his seat on the box Mr. Treadman leaned over towards the fly.

'Lord, I entreat You to honour with Your presence the habitation of Your very daughter, Miriam Powell, whose good works, done in Your name, shine in the eyes of all men.'

He replied:

'Thy will, not Mine, be done!' Mr. Treadman shouted to the people: 'My friends, I am authorised by the Lord to announce that He will rest in the house of His faithful servant, Miriam Powell, whose name, as a single-minded labourer in Christ's vineyard, is so well-known to all of you. To mark our sense of His appreciation of the manner in which Mrs. Powell has borne the heat and burden of the day, let us join in singing that beautiful hymn which has comforted so many of us when the hours of darkness were drawing nigh, "Abide with me, fast fall the eventide."'

Mrs. Powell's house was in Maida Vale. It was late when the procession arrived. Even then it was some time before the fly could gain the house itself. The crowd had been recruited from a less desirable element since its advent in the streets of London, and this reinforcement was disposed to show something of its more disreputable side. The vehicle, with its weary horse and country driver, had to force its way through a scuffling, howling mob. For some moments it looked as if, unless the police arrived immediately in great force, there would be mischief done; until the Stranger, standing up in the fly, raised His hand, saying:

'I pray you, be still.'

And they were still. And He passed through the midst of them, with the charcoal-burner and the lame man. Mr. Treadman came after.

When He entered the house, He sighed.

Now Mrs. Powell, when she had learned that the Stranger was to be her guest, had hastened home to make ready for His coming, so that the table was set for a meal. But when He saw that there was a place for only one, He asked:

'What is this? Is there none that would eat with me?'

Mr. Treadman answered:

'Nay, Lord, there is none that is worthy. Suffer us first to wait upon You. Then afterwards we will eat also.'

He said:

'Does not a father eat with his children? Are they not of him? If there is any in this house that calls upon My name, let him sit down with me and eat.'

So they sat down and ate together. While they continued at table but little was said; for the day had been a long one, and they were weary. When they had eaten, the Stranger was shown into the best room, where was a bed which offered a pleasant resting-place for tired limbs. But He did not lie on it, nor sought repose, but went here and there about the room, as if His mind were troubled. And He cried aloud:

'Father, is it for this I came?'

In the street were heard the voices of the people, and those that cried:

'Christ has come again!'

And in the best room of the house the Stranger wept, lamenting:

'I have come unto Mine own, and Mine own know Me not. They make a mock of Me, and say, He shall be as we would have Him; we will not have Him as He is. They have made unto themselves graven images, not fashioned alike, but each an image of his own, and each would have Me to be like unto the image which he has made. For they murmur among themselves: It is we that have made God; it is not God that has made us.'

Chapter XIV

The Words of the Wise

There began to be in London that night a feeling of unrest. A sense of uncertainty came into men's minds, a desire to find answers to the questions which each asked of the other:

'Who is this man? Who does he pretend to be? Where does he come from? What does he want?'

In the minds of some that last inquiry assumed a different form. They asked, of their own hearts, if not of one another:

'Why has he come to trouble us?'

The usual showed signs of the unusual. In a great city a divergence from the normal means disturbance; which is to be avoided. When the multitude is strongly stirred by a consciousness of the abnormal in its midst, to someone, or to something, it means danger. Order is not preserved by authority, but by tradition. A suspicion that events are about to happen which are contrary to established order shakes that tradition, with the immediate result that confusion threatens.

There was that night hardly one person who was not conscious of more or less vague mental disturbance. There were those who at once leaped to the conclusion that the words of Scripture, as they interpreted them, were about to receive complete illustration. There were others whose theological outlook was capable of less mathematically accurate definition, who were yet in doubt as to whether some supernatural being might not have appeared among men. There was that large class which, having no logical grounds for expectation, is always looking for the unexpected, ever eager to believe it is upon them. The members of this class are not interested in current theories of a deity; they are indifferent whether God is or is not. The phrase 'a Second Coming' conveyed no meaning to their minds. They would welcome any new thing, whether it was Christ Jesus or Tom Fool; though, when they realised who Christ Jesus was, their preference would be strongly in favour of Tom Fool. It was, for the most part, individuals of this sort who bent their steps towards the house in which the Stranger was, and, by way of diversion, loitered in its neighbourhood throughout the night.

In the house itself a consultation was being held. Various persons who take a notorious interest in subjects of the hour were gathered together, like bees about a flower, desirous to extract from the occasion such honey as they could. Mr. Treadman, who presided, had explained to the meeting, in words which burned, what a matter of capital importance it was which had brought them there.

Professor Wilcox Wilson displayed his usual fondness for destructive criticism.

'Our friend Treadman speaks of the frightful consequences which would attend an only partial recognition of the Lord's divinity. He says nothing of the at least equally bad results which would ensue from giving credit to an impostor. Apart from the fact that there are those who are still in doubt as to which portion of the New Testament narrative is to be regarded as mythical—'

Mr. Treadman sprang to his feet.

'Mr. Wilson, this meeting is for believers only. We are not here for an academical discussion; we are here as children of Christ.'

'Quite so. I, also, am anxious to be a child of Christ. I only say, with another, "Help Thou my unbelief." It seems to me that the personage whom we will call our distinguished visitor—'

'Wilson, sit down! In my presence you shall not speak with such flippancy of the Lord Christ. It is to protest against such frames of mind that we are here. Don't you realise that He who is in the room above us has but to lift His little finger to lay you dead?'

'It would prove nothing if he did; certainly not that he is the Lord Christ. My dear Treadman, let me ask you seriously to consider whether you propose to conduct your crusade on logical lines or as creatures of impulse. If it is as the latter you intend to figure, you will do an incalculable amount of mischief. The Lord who made us is aware of our deficiencies. He is responsible for them.'

'No! No!'

'Who, then, is? Is there a greater than God? Do you blaspheme? He knows that He has given us, as one of the strongest passions of our nature, a craving for demonstrable proof. If this is shown in little things, then how much more in greater! If you want it proved that two and two are five, then are you not equally desirous of having it clearly established that a wandering stranger has claims to call himself divine? So put, the question answers itself. If this man is God, he will have no difficulty in demonstrating the fact beyond all possibility of doubt; and he will demonstrate it, for he knows that human nature, for which he is responsible, requires such demonstration. If he does not, then rest assured he is no God.'

Mr. Jebb stood up.

'What sort of proof does Professor Wilson require? What amount would he esteem sufficient? Would he expect that the demonstration should be repeated in the case of each separate individual? I put these questions, feeling that the Professor has possibly his own point of view, because it is asserted that miracles have taken place. A large body of apparently trustworthy evidence testifies to the fact. I am bound to admit that my own researches go to show that the occurrences in question are at least extra-natural. Does the Professor suggest that any power short of what we call Divine can go outside nature?'

The Professor replied:

'I will be candid, and confess that it is because the events referred to are of so extraordinary a nature that I am in this galley. I have hitherto seen no reason to doubt that everything which has happened in cosmogony is capable of a natural explanation. If I am to admit the miraculous, I find myself confronted by new conditions, on which account I ask this worker of wonders to show who and what he is.'

'He has already shown Himself to be more than man.'

'I grant that he has shown himself to be a remarkable person. But it does not by any means therefore follow that he is the Son of God, the Christ of tradition.'

Mr. Treadman broke into the discussion.

'He has shown Himself to me to be the Christ.'

'But how? that's what I don't understand. How?'

'Wilson, pray that one day He may show Himself to you before it is too late. Pray! pray! then you'll understand the how, wherefore, and why, though you'll still not be able to express them in the terms of a scientific formula.'

The Professor shrugged his shoulders.

'That is the sort of talk which has been responsible for the superstition which has been the world's greatest bane. The votaries of the multifarious varieties of hanky-panky have always shown a distaste for the cold, dry light of truth, which is all that science is.'

Jebb smiled.

'I am not so exigent as the Professor. I recognise the presence in our midst of a worker of wonders—a god among men. And although in that latter phrase some may only see a poetic license, I am disposed to be content. For I represent a too obvious fact—the fact that one portion of the world is the victim of the other part's injustice. As I came here to-night I passed through men and women, ragged, tattered, and torn, smirched with all manner of uncleanliness, who were hastening towards this house as if towards the millennium. Remembering how often that quest had been a dream, I asked myself if it were possible that at last it gleamed on the horizon. As I put to myself the question, my heart leaped up into my mouth. For it was borne in upon me, as a thing not to be denied, that it might be that, in the best of all possible senses, the Day of the Lord has arrived—the Great Day of the Lord.'

'It has arrived, Jebb, be sure of it!'

'I think—I say it with all due deference—that it will not be our fault if it has not, in the sense in which I use the phrase. I am told that we have Christ again among us. On that pronouncement I pass no opinion. I stand simply for those that suffer. I do know that we are in actual touch with one who has given proofs of his capacity to alleviate pain and make glad the sorrowful. Experience has shown that by nothing less than a miracle can the submerged millions be raised out of the depths. Here is a doer of miracles. Already he has shown that a cry of anguish gains access to the heart, and impels him to a removal of the cause. Here is a great healer, the physician the world is so much in want of. Would it not be well for us, sinking all controversial differences, to join hands in approaching him, and in showing him, with all humility, the wounds which gape widest, and the souls which are enduring most, doing this in the trust that the sight of so much affliction will quicken his sympathies, and move him to right the wrong, and to make the rough ways smooth? How he will do it I cannot say. But he who can raise a cancerous corpse from an operating table, and endue it with life and health upon the instant, can do that and more. To such an one all things are possible. I ask you to consider whether it will not be well that we should discuss the best and most effective manner in which, in the morning, this matter can be laid before him who has come among us.'

Scarcely had Mr. Jebb ceased to speak than there rose a huge man, with matted beard, untidy hair, eager eyes, and a voice which seemed to shake the room. This was the socialist, Henry Walters. He spoke with tumultuous haste, as if it was all he could do to keep up with the words which came rushing along his tongue.

'I say, Yes! if that's the Christ you're talking about, I'm for him. If this disturber of the peace is a creature with red blood in his veins, count me on his side. For he'll be a disturber of the peace with a vengeance. If at last Heaven has given us someone who is prepared to deal, not with abstractions, but with facts, then I cry: "Hallelujah for the King of Kings!" For it's more important that our rookeries should be made decent dwelling-places than that all the Churches should plump for the Thirty-nine Articles. The prospect of a practical Christ almost turns my brain. Religion is a synonym for contradiction in theory and practice, but a Christ who is a live man, and not a decoration for an altarpiece, will be likely to have clear notions on the problems which are beyond our finding out, and to care little for singing bad verses about the golden sea. We want a Saviour more than the handful of Jews did, who at least had breathing space in the 11,000 miles of open country, with a respectable climate, which you call Palestine. But he must be a Saviour that is a Saviour; not an utterer of dark sayings which are made darker by being interpreted, but a doer of deeds. Let him purify the moral and physical atmosphere of a single London alley, and he'll not want for followers. Let him assure the London dockers of a decent return for honest labour, and he'll write his name for all time on their hearts. Let him put an end to sweating, and explain to the wicked mighty that by right their seats should be a little lower down, and he'll have all that's worth having in the world upon his side. You talk about a Saviour of the poor. If such an one has come at last, the face of this country will be transformed in a fashion which will surprise some of you who live on the poor. There'll be no need of a second crucifixion, or for more tittle-tattle about dying for sinners. Let him live for them. He has but to choose to conquer, to will to extend his empire, eternally, from pole to pole. And since these are my sentiments I need not enlarge on the zest with which I shall join in the discussion suggested by Mr. Jebb as to the most irresistible method of laying before him who has come among us the plain fact that this chaos called a city is but a huge charnel-house of human misery.'

When Mr. Walters sat down the Rev. Martin Philipps rose:

'I have listened in silence to the remarks which we have just heard because I felt that this was preeminently an occasion on which every man, conscious of his own responsibility, was entitled to an uninterrupted exposition of his views, however abhorrent those views might be to some of us. I need not tell you how both the tone and spirit of those to which we have just been listening are contrary to every sense and fibre of my being. Mr. Jebb and the last speaker seem only to see the secular side of the subject which is before us. This is the more surprising as it has no secular side. If Christ has come, it is as a Divinity, not as an adherent of this or that political or social school, but as an intermediary between heaven and earth. I cannot express to you the horror with which I regard the notion that the purport of His presence here can be to administer to the material wants of men. To suppose so is indeed to mock God. We as Christians know better. It is our blessed privilege to be aware that it is not our bodies which He seeks, but our souls. Our body is but the envelope which contains the soul, and from which one day it emerges, like the chrysalis from the cocoon. The one endures but for a few years, the other through all eternity.

'I would not inflict on you these platitudes were it not necessary, after the remarks which we have heard, for us, as Christians to make our position plain. If Christ has come again, it is in infinite love, to make a further effort to save us from the consequences of our own sin, to complete the work of His atonement, and to seek once more to gather us within the safety of His fold.

'I had never thought that under any possible circumstances I should be constrained to ask myself the question, Has Christ come again? Strange human blindness! I had always supposed that, as a believer in Christ, and Him crucified, and as a preacher, I should never have the slightest doubt as to whether or not He had returned to earth. I see now with clearer eyes; I perceive my own poor human frailty; I realise more clearly the nature of the puzzle which must have presented itself to the Jews of old. I use the word "puzzle" because it seems to define the situation more accurately than any other which occurs to me. Looking back across the long tale of the years, it is difficult for us to properly apprehend the full bearing of the fact that Christ, the Son of God, was once an ordinary man, in manners, habits, and appearance exactly like ourselves. We say glibly: "He was made man," but how many of us stop to realise what, in their entirety, those words mean! When I first heard that someone was in London who, it was rumoured, was the Lord Jesus, my feeling was one of shock, horror, amazement, to think that anyone could be guilty of so blasphemous a travesty. If you consider, probably the same sensation was felt by Jews who were told that the Messiah, to whose advent their whole history pointed, was in their midst. When they were shown an ordinary man, who to their eyes looked exactly like his fellows—a person of absolutely no account whatever—their feeling was one of deep disgust, derision, scorn, which presently became fanatical rage. Exactly what they were looking for, more or less vaguely (for the promise was of old, and the performance long delayed), they scarcely knew themselves. But it was not this. Who is this man? What is his name? Where does he come from? What right has he to hold himself up as different from us? These were questions which they asked. When the answers came their rage grew more, until the sequel was the hill of Calvary.

'A similar problem confronts us today in London. We believe in Christ, although we never saw Him. I sometimes think that, if we had seen Him, we might not have believed. God grant that I am wrong! For nearly nineteen hundred years we have watched and waited for His Second Coming. The time has been long; the disappointments have been many, until at last there has grown up in the midst of some a sort of dull wonder as to whether He will ever come again at all. "How long?" many of us have cried—"O Lord, how long?" Suddenly our question receives an answer of a sort. We are told: "No longer—now. The great day of the Lord is already here. Christ has come again." When in our bewilderment we ask, "Where is He? What is He like? Whence has He come, and how? Why wholly unannounced, in such guise and fashion?" we receive the same answer as did the Jews of old.

'This is a grave matter which we have met to discuss—so grave that I hardly dare to speak of it; but this I will venture to say: I know that my Redeemer liveth; but whether I should know Him, as He should be known, if I met Him face to face, very man of very man, here upon earth, I cannot certainly say. I entreat God to forgive me in that I am compelled, to my shame, to make such a confession; and I believe that He will forgive me, for He knows, as none else can, how strange a thing is the heart of man. He who is with us in this house tonight has been spoken of as a worker of wonders. That I myself know he is, and of wonders which are other than material. When yesterday I stood before him, I was abashed. The longer I stayed, the more my sense of self-abasement grew. I felt as if I, a thing of impurity, had been brought into sudden, unexpected contact with one who was wholly pure. I was ashamed. I am conscious that there is a presence in this house which, though intangible, is not to be denied. Whether or not the physical form and shape of our Lord is in the room above us, He is present in our midst; and I confidently hope, when I have sought guidance from God in prayer—as I trust that we presently shall all do—to obtain light from the Fountain of all light which shall make clear to me the way.'

The Rev. Martin Philipps was succeeded by Mr. John Anthony Gibbs. Mr. Gibbs was a short, portly person, with a manner which suggested, probably in spite of himself, a combination of the pedagogue with the man of business.

'I believe that I am entitled to say that I represent certain religious bodies in the present House of Commons, and while endorsing what the last speaker has said, I would add to his remarks one or two of my own. I apprehend that it is generally allowed that we have among us a remarkable man. I understand that he is with us to-night beneath this very roof. The spirit of the age is inclined towards incredulity, but I for one am disposed to be convinced that he is not as others are. Admitting the bare possibility of his being more than man, even though he be less than God, I confidently affirm that it is to the Churches first of all that the question is of primary importance. I would suggest that representations be at once made to the different Churches.'

'Including the Roman Catholic?'

The question came from Henry Walters.

'No, sir; not to the Roman Catholic hierarchy; I was speaking of the Christian Churches only.'

'And the Roman Catholic is not one of them?'

'Most emphatically not, as it is within the bounds of possibility that it will speedily and finally learn. I speak for the Churches of Protestant Christendom only.'

'That is very good of you.'

'And I repeat that I would suggest that representations should be made to those that are in authority, and that meetings be called; a first to be attended by the clergy only, and a second by both the clergy and laity, at which this great question should be properly and adequately discussed.'

'And what's to happen in the meantime?'

'Sir, I was not addressing you.'

'But I was addressing you. We all know what religious meetings are like, especially when they are attended by representatives of Protestant Christendom only. While they are making up their minds about the differences between Tweedledum and Tweedledee, is Christ, humbly quiescent, to stand awaiting their decision?'

'Sir, your language is repulsive. I am only addressing myself to those persons present who are proud to call themselves Christians. And them I am asking to consider whether it is not in the highest degree advisable that we should endeavour to obtain at the earliest possible moment the opinion of our bishops and clergy on this question of the most supreme importance.'

'Hear, hear! And when we've got them, we shall know how to appreciate them at their proper value. The Lord deliver us from our bishops and clergy!'

After Mr. Gibbs had resumed his seat there ensued an interval, during which no one evinced an inclination to continue the discussion. Possibly Mr. Walters's interruptions had not inspired anyone with a desire to incur his criticism. His voice and manner were alike obstreperous. There were those present who knew from experience that it was extremely difficult to shout him down.

When some moments had passed without the silence being broken, Mr. Treadman leaned across the table towards where sat that singular personality whose name is a synonym for the Salvation Army, and who has credited himself with brevet rank as 'General' Robins.

'General, is there nothing which you wish to say to us? Surely this is not a subject on which you would desire to have your voice unheard?'

The 'General' was sitting right back in his chair. He was an old man. The suggestion of age was accentuated by his attitude. His back was bowed, his head hung forward on his chest, his hands lay on his knees, as if the arms to which they were attached were limp and weary. He did not seem to be aware that he was being addressed, so that Mr. Treadman had to repeat his question. When it was put a second time he glanced up with a start, as if he had been brought back with a shock from the place of shadows in which his thoughts had been straying.

'I was thinking,' he replied.

'Of what? Will you not allow us to hear our thoughts on a subject whose magnitude bulks larger with each word we utter?'

The old man was silent, as if he were considering. Then he said, without altering his position:

'I was thinking that I knew more when I was young than I do now that I am old. All my life I have been sure—till now. Now, the first time that assurance is really needed, it is gone, and has left me troubled. God help us all!'

'Explain yourself, General.'

'That's another part of the trouble, that I'm pretty nearly afraid to explain. All the days of my life I've been crying: "Take courage! Put doubt behind you!" And now, when courage is what I most am wanting, it's fled; only doubt remains.'

'But, General, you of all others have no cause for doubt; and you've proved your courage on a hundred fields. You've not only fought the good fight yourself, you have shown others how to fight it too.'

'That's it—have I? As Mr. Philipps said, to-night there's a Presence in the air, I felt It as I came up the street, as I entered this house, and more and more as I've been seated in this room. And in that Presence I have grown afraid, fearful lest in all that I have done I have done wrong. I confess—because It knows—that I have had doubts as to the propriety of my proceedings from the first. Like Saul, I seem to have been smitten with sudden blindness in order that I may see at last. I see that what Christ wants is not what I have given Him. I understood man's nature, but refused to understand His. I realised that there is nothing like sensationalism to attract a certain sort of men and women; I declined to realise that it does not attract Christ. Confident assertion pleases the mob, when it's in a certain humour, but not Him. Bands, uniforms, newspapers, catchwords—all the machinery of advertisement I have employed;—but He does not advertise. Worst of all, I've taught from a thousand platforms that a man may be a notorious sinner one minute and a child of Christ the next. I know that is not so.'

The old man stood up, his quavering tones rising in a shrill crescendo.

'You ask me to tell you what I think. I think that we are about to stand before the judgment-seat of God as doomed men. We have been like the Scribes and Pharisees, saying, We know Christ, and are therefore not as others, when all the time our knowledge has been hurrying us not to but from Him. I know that my Redeemer liveth, and have used that knowledge for my own ends. Because it seemed to me that His methods were ineffective, I have said, Not His will, but mine be done. I have taught Him, not as He would be taught, but as it has suited me to teach Him. I have lied of Him and to Him, and have taught a great multitude to lie also. I have made of Him a mockery in the eyes of men, dragged Him through the gutter, flaunted Him from the hoardings, used Him as a street show, and as a mountebank in the houses which I have called not His, but mine. I have blasphemed His Name by using it as a meaningless catch-phrase in the foolish mouths of men and women seeking for a new sensation, or for self-display. I have done all these things and many more. I am an old man. What time have I for atonement? For I know now that what Christ wants is a man's life, not merely a part of it—the beginning, the middle, or the end. You cannot win him with a phrase in a moment of emotion. You have gradually, persistently, quietly, to mould yourself in His image. Nothing else will serve. For that, for me, the time is past. I cannot undo what I have done, nor can I begin again. It is too late.

'You ask me what I think. I think if Christ has come again—I fear He has, for strange things have happened to me since I entered the Presence that is in this room—that we had better flee, though where, I do not know; for wherever we go we shall take Him with us. I, for one, dare not meet Him face to face. I envy him his courage that dare, though he will have to be made of different stuff from any of us if it is to avail him anything. Be assured of this, that for us the Second Coming will not be a joyful advent. It will mean, at best, the pricking of the bubbles we have so long and so laboriously been blowing. We shall be made to know ourselves as He knows us. There will be the beginning of the end. What form that end will take I dare not endeavour to foresee. God help us all!'

There was a curious quality in the silence that ensued when the 'General' ceased, until Mr. Treadman sprang to his feet.

'I protest, with all the strength that is in me, against the doctrine which we have just heard! It is abominable—a thing of horror—contrary to all that we know of God's love and His infinite mercy! I know that it is false!'

'Oh, man! man! it's few things we haven't known, you and I—except ourselves. And that knowledge is coming to us too soon. Woeful will be the day!'

'I cannot but think that the sudden rush of exciting events has turned our honoured friend's brain.'

'It has, towards the light; so that I can see the outer darkness which lies beyond.'

'General, I cannot find language with which to express the pain I feel at the tendency which I perceive in your attitude to turn your back on all the teachings of your life.'

'Your sentence is involved—your sentences sometimes are; but your meaning's tolerably clear. I'm sorry too.'

'Do you mean to deny that he who repents finds God—you who have been vehement in the cause of instant conversion.'

'To my shame you say it.'

'Your shame! Have you forgotten that there is more joy in heaven over one sinner that repenteth than over ninety-nine just persons? You out-Herod Calvin in his blackest moods.'

'I'll not dispute with you. It's but words, words. I only hope that by repentance He means what you do. But I greatly fear.'

'I am sure.'

'Oh, man, how often we have been sure—we two!'

'I am sure still. My friends, the General is nearer to Christ than he thinks, and Christ is nearer to him. We shall do no harm, any of us, by expressing our consciousness of sin, though at such a time as this I cannot but think that such an expression may go too far. We who are here have all of us laboured in our several ways in the Lord's vineyard. To suggest that the fruit of our endeavours has been all that it might have been would be presumption. We are but men. The best that men can do is faulty. But we have done our best, each according to his or her light. And having done that best, we are entitled to wait with a glad confidence the inspection of the Master. To suppose that He will require from us what He knows it has not been in our power to give or to do—I thank God that there is nothing in Scripture or out of it to cause any one to imagine that He is so relentless a taskmaster. And I—I have enjoyed the glad and glorious privilege of standing in His very presence. I have dared to speak to Him, to look Him in the face. I give you my personal assurance that I have not suffered for my daring, but have been filled instead with a great joy, and with an infinite content. No, General; no, my friends; the Lord has not come to us in anger, but in peace—a man like unto ourselves, knowing our infirmities, to wipe the tears out of our eyes. Do not, I beseech you, look upon Him for a moment as the dreadful being the General has depicted. The General himself, when his black mood has passed, and he finds himself indeed face to face with his Master, will be the first to perceive how contrary to truth that picture is. And in that moment he will know, once and forever, how very certain it is that the Second Coming of our Lord and Saviour is to us, His children, an occasion of great joy.'

Chapter XV

The Supplicant

There was in the house that night one person who did not attempt to sleep—its mistress, Mrs. Miriam Powell, a woman of character; a fact which was sufficiently demonstrated by the name by which she was best known to the world. For when the Christian name of a married woman is familiar to the public it is because she is a person of marked individuality.

Something of her history was notorious; not only within a large circle of acquaintance, but outside of it. It had lost nothing in the telling. An unhappy marriage; a loose-living husband—a man who was in more senses than one unclean; a final resolution on her part to live out her life alone. Out of these data she had evolved a set of opinions on sexual questions to which she endeavoured to induce anyone and everyone, in season and out of season, to listen. There were some who regarded her with sympathy, some with admiration, some with respect, and some with fatigue.

In such cases women are apt to be regarded as representatives of a class; as abstractions, not concrete facts. The accident of her having had a bad husband was known to all the world; that she was herself the victim of a temperament was not. She was of the stuff out of which saints and martyrs may have been made, which is not necessarily good material out of which to make a wife. Enthusiasm was a necessity of her existence—not the frothy, fleeting frenzy of a foolish female, but an enduring possession of the kind which makes nothing of fighting with beasts at Ephesus. Although she herself might not be aware of it, the nature of her matrimonial experiences had given her what her instincts craved for: a creed—sexual reform.

She maintained that sexual intercourse was a thing of horror; the cause of all the evil which the world contains. Although she was wise enough not to proclaim the fact, in her heart she was of opinion that it would be better that the race should die out rather than that the evil should continue. She aimed at what she called universal chastity; maintaining that the less men and women had to do with each other the better. In pursuit of this chimera she performed labours which, if not worthy of Hercules, at least resembled those of Sisyphus in that they had to be done over and over again. The stone would not stay at the top of the hill.

At the outset she had been convinced—as the fruit of her own experience—that the fault lay with the men. Latterly she had been inclining more and more to the belief that the women had something to do with it as well. Indeed, she was beginning to more than suspect that theirs might be the major part of the blame. The suspicion filled her with a singular sort of rage.

This was the person to whose house the Stranger had come at this particular stage of her mental development. His advent had brought her to the verge of what is called madness in the case of an ordinary person of today; and spiritual exaltation in the case of saints and martyrs. She already knew that she was on a hopeless quest, and, although the fact did not daunt her for a moment, had realised that nothing short of a miracle would bring about that change in the human animal which she desired. Here was the possibility of a miracle actually at hand. Here was a worker of wonders—men said, the very Christ.

It was the reflection that what men said might be true which made her courage quail at last.

A miracle-monger she desired. But—the Christ! To formulate the proposition which was whirling in her brain to a doer-of-strange-deeds was one thing, but—to Him! That was another.

When she had come into His near neighbourhood she had shrunk back, a frightened creature. She had been afraid to look Him in the face. Ever since He had been beneath her roof she had been shaken as with palsy.

Dare she do this thing?

That was the problem which had been present in her mind the whole day long, and which still racked it in the silent watches of the night. To and fro she passed, from room to room, from floor to floor. More than once she approached the door behind which He was, only to start away from it again and flee. She did not even dare to kneel at His portal, fearful lest He, knowing she was there, might come out and see. In her own chamber she scanned the New Testament in search of words which would comfort and encourage her. In vain. The sentences seemed to rise up from off the printed pages to condemn her.

She had an idea. The lame man and the charcoal-burner were the joint occupants of a spare room. She would learn from them what manner of man their Master was—whether He might be expected to lend a sympathetic ear to such a supplication as that which she had it in her heart to make. But when she stood outside their apartment she reflected that they were common fellows. Her impulse had been to refuse them shelter, being at a loss to understand what connection there could be between her guest and such a pair. That they had thrust themselves upon Him she thought was probable; the more reason, therefore, why she should decline to countenance their presumptuous persistence. To seek from them advice or information would be an act of condescension which would be as resultless as undignified.

No. Better go directly to the fountainhead. That would be the part both of propriety and wisdom.

She screwed her courage to the sticking-point, and went.

The two disciples were lodged in an upper story. She had her knuckles against the panel of their door when at last her resolution was arrived at. Straightway relinquishing her former purpose, she hastened down the stairs to the floor on which He was. As she went the clock in the hall struck three.

The announcement of the hour moved her to fresh irresolution. Would it be seemly to rouse Him out of slumber to press on Him such a petition? Yet if she did not do it now, when could she? She might never again have such an opportunity. Were His ears not always open to the prayers of those that stood in need of help? What difference did the night or the morning make to Him? She put out her hand towards the door.

As she did so a great fear came over her. It was as though she was stricken with paralysis. She could neither do as she intended nor withdraw her hand. She remained as one rooted to the floor. How long she stayed she did not know. The seconds and the minutes passed, and still she did not move. Presently her fear grew greater. She knew, although she had not made a sound, that, conscious of her presence, He was coming towards her on the other side of the door.

Then the door was opened, and she saw Him face to face. He did not speak a word; and she was still. The gift of fluent speech for which she was notorious had gone from her utterly. He looked at her in such fashion that she was compelled to meet His eyes, though she would have given all that she had to have been able to escape their scrutiny. For in them was an eloquence which was not of words, and a quality which held her numb. For she was conscious not only that He knew her, in a sense of which she had never dreamed in her blackest nightmares, but that He was causing her to know herself. In the fierce light of that self-knowledge her heart dried up within her. She saw herself as what she was—the embittered, illiberal, narrow-minded woman who, conscious of her isolation, had raised up for herself a creed of her own—a creed which was not His. She saw how, with the passage of the years, her persistence in this creed had forced her farther and farther away from Him, until now she had grown to have nothing in common with Him, since she had so continually striven to bring about the things which He would not have. She had placed herself in opposition to His will, and now had actually come to solicit His endorsement of her action. And she knew that in so doing she had committed the greatest of all her sins.

She did not offer her petition. But when the door was closed again, and He had passed from her actual sight, there stood without one from whose veins the wine of life had passed, and whose hair had become white as snow. Although not a word had been spoken, she had stood before the Judgment Seat, and tasted of more than the bitterness of death. When she began to return to her own room she had to feel her way with her hands. Her sight had become dim, her limbs feeble. She had grown old.

Chapter XVI

In the Morning

All through the night people remained in the street without. With the return of day their numbers so increased that the authorities began to be concerned. The house itself was besieged. It was with difficulty that the police could keep a sufficient open space in front to enable persons to pass in and out. An official endeavoured to represent to the inmates the authoritative point of view.

'Whose house is this?' he asked of the servant who opened the door.

He was told.

'Can I see Mrs. Powell?'

The maid seemed bewildered.

'We don't know what's the matter with her. We're going to send for a doctor.'

'Is she ill?'

'She's grown old since last night.'

'What do you mean?'

The officer stared. The girl began to cry.

'I want to get away. I'm frightened.'

'Don't be silly. What have you got to be frightened at? Can't I see someone who's responsible? I don't know who you've got in the house, but whoever it is, he'd better go before there's trouble.'

'They say it's Christ.'

'Christ or no Christ, I tell you he'd better go somewhere where his presence won't be the occasion of a nuisance. Is there no one I can see?'

'I am here.' The answer came from Mr. Treadman, who, with three other persons, had just entered the hall. 'What is it, constable? Is there anything you want?'

'I don't know who you are, sir, but if you're the cause of the confusion outside you're incurring a very serious responsibility.'

'I am not the cause; it is not me they have come to see. They have come to see the Lord. Officer, Christ has come again.'

Mr. Treadman laid his hand upon the official's arm; who instantly shook it off again.

'I know nothing about that; I want to know nothing. I only know that no one has a right to cause a nuisance.'

'Cause a nuisance? Christ! Officer, are you mad?'

'I don't want to talk to you. I have my instructions; they're enough for me. My instructions are to see that the nuisance is abated. The best way to do that is to induce your friend to take himself somewhere else without any fuss.' Voices came from the street. 'Do you hear that? A lot of half-witted people have foolishly brought their sick friends, and have actually got them out there, as if this was some sort of hospital at which medical attendance could be had for the asking. If anything happens to those sick people, it won t be nice for whoever is to blame.'

'Nothing will happen. The Lord has only to raise His hand, to say the word, for them to be made whole. They know it; their faith has made them sure.'

The officer regarded the other for a moment or two before he spoke again.

'Look here, I don't know what your game is—'

'Game?'

'And I don't know what new religion it is you're supposed to be teaching—'

'New religion? The religion we are teaching is as old as the hills.'

'Very well; then that's all right. You take it to the hills; there'll be more room there. You tell your friend that the sooner he takes a trip into the country the better it'll be for everyone concerned.'

'Officer, don't you understand what it means when you are told that Christ has come again? Can it be possible that you are not a Christian?'

The official waved his hand.

'The only thing about which I'm concerned is my duty, and my duty is to carry out my instructions. If, as I say, your friend is a sensible man, he'll change his quarters as soon as he possibly can. You'll find me waiting outside, to know what he intends to do. Don't keep me any longer than you can help.'

The official's disappearance was followed by a momentary silence; then Mr. Treadman laughed awkwardly, as if his sense of humour had been tickled by something which was not altogether pleasant.

'That is the latest touch of irony, that Christ should be regarded as a common nuisance, and on His Second Coming to be the Judge of all the earth requested to take Himself elsewhere!'

The Rev. Martin Philipps pursed his lips.

'What you say is correct enough; it is a ludicrous notion. But, on the other hand, the position is not a simple one. If, as they bid fair to do, the people flock here in huge crowds, at the very least there will be confusion, and the police will have difficulty in keeping order.'

'You would not have the people refrain from coming to greet their Lord?'

'I would nave them observe some method. Do you yourself wish that they should press upon Him in an unmanageable mob?'

'Have no fear of that. He will hold them in the hollow of His hand, and will see that they observe all the method that is needed. For my part, I'd have them flock to Him from all the corners of the earth—and they will.'

'In that case I trust that they will not endeavour to pack themselves within the compass of the London streets.'

'Be at peace, my friend; do not let yourself be troubled. All that He shall do will be well. Now, first, to see our dear sister, whose request He granted, and whom He so greatly blessed by staying beneath her roof.'

As he spoke, turning, he saw a figure coming down the stairs—an old woman, who tottered from tread to tread, clinging to the banister, as if she needed it both as a guide and a support.

'Who is this?' he asked. Then: 'It can't be Mrs. Powell?' It was. He ran to her. 'My dear friend, what has happened to you since I saw you last?'

The old woman, grasping the banister with both hands, looked down at him.

'I have seen Him face to face!'

'Seen whom?'

'Christ. I have stood before the judgment-seat of God.'

There was a quality in her voice which, combined with the singularity and even horror of her appearance, caused them to stare at her with doubting eyes. Mr. Treadman put a question to the servant, who still lingered in the passage:

'What does she mean? What has taken place?'

The girl began again to whimper.

'I don't know. I want to go—I daren't stop—I'm frightened!'

Mr. Treadman ascended to the old woman.

'Take my arm; let me help you down, then you can tell me all that has happened.'

With her two hands she caught his arm in a convulsive grip. At her touch they saw that his countenance changed. As they descended side by side upon his face was a curious expression, almost as if he was afraid of his companion. As she came the others retreated. When he led her into a room the others followed at a distance, showing a disposition to linger in the doorway. He brought her to a chair.

'Here is a seat. Sit down.'

She glanced with her dim eyes furtively to the front and back, to the right and left, continuing to clutch his arm, as if unwilling to relinquish its protection. He was obviously embarrassed.

'Did you not hear what I said? Here is a seat. Let me go.'

She neither answered nor showed any signs of releasing him. He called to those in the doorway:

'Come and help me, someone; she grips my arm as in a vice. Mrs. Powell, I must insist upon your doing as I request. Let me go!'

With a sudden wrench he jerked himself away. Deprived of his support, she dropped on to the ground. Indifferent to her apparent helplessness, he hurried to the trio at the door.

'There's something awful about her—worse than madness. She has given me quite a nervous shock.'

'General' Robins answered; he was one of the three who had come with Mr. Treadman.

'As she herself says, she has seen Him face to face. Wait till we also have seen Him face to face. God help us all!'

The Rev. Martin Philipps fidgeted.

'Without wishing to countenance any extravagant theories, it is plain that something very strange has happened to Mrs. Powell. I trust that we ourselves are incurring no unnecessary risks.'

Mr. Jebb, who also had come with Mr. Treadman, regarded the speaker in a manner which was not flattering.

'You religious people are always thinking of yourselves. It is because you are afraid of what will happen to what you call your souls that you try to delude yourselves with the pretence that you believe; regarding faith as a patent medicine warranted to cure all ills. You might find indifference to self a safer recipe.'

Picking up Mrs. Powell from where she still lay upon the floor, he placed her in a chair.

'My good lady, the proper place for you is in bed.' He called to the maid: 'See that your mistress is put to bed at once, and a doctor sent for.'

'A doctor,' cried Mr. Treadman, 'when the Great Healer Himself is upstairs!'

'You appear to ignore the fact that, according to your creed, the Great Healer, as you call him, metes out not rewards only, but punishments as well. He is not a doctor to whom you have only to offer a fee to command his services.'

'General' Robins caught at the words.

'He does ignore it; and by his persistence in so doing he makes our peril every moment greater.'

'At the same time,' continued Mr. Jebb, 'it is just as well that we should keep our heads. A person of Mrs. Powell's temperament and history may pass from what she was to what she is in the twinkling of an eye without the intervention of anything supernatural. So much is certain.'

Mr. Treadman, who had been wiping his brow with his pocket-handkerchief, as if suffering from a sudden excess of heat, joined in the conversation.

'My dear friend, God moves in a mysterious way. We all know that. Let us not probe into His actions in this or that particular instance, but rest content with the general assurance that all things work together for the good of those that love the Lord. Let us not forget the errand which has brought us here. Let us lose no more time, but use all possible expedition in opening our hearts to Him.'

'I wish, Treadman, since you are not a parson, that you wouldn't ape the professional twang. Isn't ordinary English good enough for you?'

'My dear Jebb, you are pleased to be critical. My sole desire is to speak of Him with all possible reverence.'

'Then be reverent in decent every-day English. Are you suggesting that we should seek his presence? Because, if so I'm ready.'

It seemed, however, that the other two were not. 'General' Robins openly confessed his unwillingness to, as he put it, meet the Stranger face to face. Nor was Mr. Philipps's eagerness in that direction much greater than his. Even Mr. Treadman showed signs of a chastened enthusiasm. It needed Mr. Jebb's acerbity to rekindle the expiring flame. Mr. Treadman repudiated the hints which his associate threw out with a show both of heat and scorn.

Soon the quartette were mounting the stairs which led to the Stranger's room. On the landing there was a pause. The 'General' and Mr. Philipps, whose unwillingness to proceed further had by no means vanished, still lagged behind. Mr. Jebb lashed them with his tongue.

'What's wrong with you? Is it spiritual fear or physical? In either case, what fine figures you both present! All these years you have been sounding your trumpets, proclaiming that you are Christ's, and Christ is yours; that the only thing for which you have yearned is His return. Now see how you shiver and shake! Is it because you are afraid that He has come, or because you fear He hasn't?'

'I don't think,' stammered Mr. Philipps, 'that you are entitled to say I am afraid—other than in the sense in which every true believer must be afraid when he finds himself standing on the threshold of the Presence.'

The 'General' was more candid.

'I fear, I fear! He knows me altogether! He knows I fear!'

Mr. Treadman endeavoured to return to his old assurance.

'Come, my friends, let us fear nothing. Whether we live we are the Lord's; or whether we die we are the Lord's, blessed be the name of the Lord! Let us rejoice and make glad, and enter into His presence with a song.'

Without knocking, turning the handle of the door in front of which they stood, he went into the room. Mr. Jebb went with him. After momentary hesitation, the Rev. Martin Philipps followed after. But

'General' Robins stayed without. It was as if he made an effort to force his feet across the threshold, and as if they refused him their obedience. The tall, rugged figure, clad in its bizarre uniform, trembled as with ague.

On a sudden one of the bands for whose existence he was responsible burst into blatant sound in the street beyond. As its inharmonious notes reached his ears, he leant forward and hid his face against the wall.

Chapter XVII

The Miracle of Healing

The Stranger was seated, conversing with His two disciples. When the trio entered He was still. From the street came the noise of the Salvation Army band and the voices of the people. There was in the air the hum of a great multitude.

Something of his assurance had gone from Mr. Treadman. His tongue was not so ready, his bearing more uncertain. When he spoke, it was with emotion which was almost tearful, at first, in gentler tones than he was wont to use.

'Lord, we Thy servants, sinners though we are, and conscious of our infirmities, come to Thee to offer up our supplications. We come in the name of Thy people. For though, like children, they have erred and strayed, and lacked the wisdom of the Father, yet they are Thy children, Lord, and hold Thy name in reverence. And they are many. In all the far places of the world they are to be found. And in this great city they are for numbers as the sands of the sea. Not all of one pattern—not all wise or strong. Associated with the various branches of the universal Church, differing in little things, they are all of one mind upon one point, their love for Thee. We pray Thee to make Thyself known to the great host which is Thy family, assuring Thee that Thou hast only to do so to find that it fills all the world. The exigencies of modern civilisation render it difficult for a mortal monarch to meet his subjects as he would desire; nor, with all respect be it urged, is the difficulty made less in the case of the King of Kings. Therefore we have ventured, subject to Thy approval, to make arrangements for the hire of a large building, called the Albert Hall, which is capable of holding several thousand persons. And we pray that Thou wilt deign to there meet detachments of Thy people in such numbers as the structure will accommodate, as a preliminary to the commencement of Thy reign over all the earth. Since the people are so anxious to see Thy face that already the police find it difficult to keep their eagerness within due bounds, we would entreat Thee to delay as little as possible, and to hold Thy first reception in the Albert Hall this afternoon. This prayer we lay at Thy feet in the hope and trust that Thou wilt not be unwilling to avail Thyself of the experience and organising powers of such of Thy servants as have spent their lives in the highways and byways of this great city, working for Thy Holy Name.'

When Mr. Treadman had finished, the Stranger asked of Mr. Jebb:

'What is it that you would say to Me?'

Mr. Jebb replied:

'I have not Mr. Treadman's command of a particular sort of language, but in a general way I would endorse all that he has said, adding a postscript for which I am alone responsible. I do not know what is the purpose of your presence here, and—with all respect to certain of my friends—I do not think that anyone else knows either. I trust that you are here for the good of the world at large, and not as the representative of this or that system of theology. Should that be the case, I would observe that sound religion is synonymous with a sound body, and that no soldier is at his best as a fighting man who is under-fed. I ask your attention to the poor of London—the materially poor. You have, I am told, demonstrated your capacity to perform miracles. If ever there was a place in which a miracle was required, it is the city of London. Cleanse the streets, purify the dwellings, clothe the poor, put food into their bellies, make it possible for them to live like decent men and women, and you will raise an enduring monument to the honour and glory of God. The human family has shown itself incapable of providing adequately for its various members. Make good that incapacity, and you will at once establish the kingdom of heaven here on earth. I ask to be allowed to place before you certain details which will illustrate some of the worst of the evils which require attention, in the belief that they have only to be brought home to you with sufficient force to be at once swept out of existence.'

The Stranger turned to the Rev. Martin Philipps.

'What is it that you would say?'

Mr. Philipps began to stammer.

'I—I had put together the heads of a few remarks which I had intended to make on this occasion, but they have all gone from me.' He stretched out his arms with a sudden cry: 'Forgive me, Lord, if in Thy presence I am dumb.'

'You have done better than these others. Is there not one who waits outside? Let him come in.'

The 'General' entered, and fell on the floor at His feet, crying, 'Lord, Lord!'

He said: 'What would you have of Me?'

'Nothing, Lord, nothing, except that You would hide from me the anger which is on Your face!'

'You also are of the company of those who would administer the kingdom of heaven as if it were their own. So that God must learn of men, not men of God! You call yourselves His children, yet seek not to know what is in the Father's heart, but exclaim of the great things which are in yours, forgetting that the wisdom of God is not as the wisdom of men. So came sin and death into the world, and still prevail. Rise. Call not so often on My Name, nor proclaim it so loudly in the market-place. Seek yourself to know Me. Take no heed to speak of Me foolishly to others, for God is sufficient unto each man for his own salvation.'

He arose, and the 'General' also. He said to Mr. Treadman and to Mr. Jebb:

'You foolish fellows! To think that God needs to be advised of men! Consider what God is; then consider what is man.' He turned to the lame man and to the charcoal-burner. 'Come! For there is that to do which must be done.'

When He had left the room the 'General' stole after Him. Mr. Jebb spoke to Mr. Treadman.

'You and I are a pair of fools!'

'Why do you say that?'

'To suppose that anything that we could say would have the slightest weight with Him. It's clearly a case of His will, not ours, be done. If tradition is to be trusted, His will was not the popular will in the days of old. He'll find that it is still less so now. Millions of men, conscious of crying grievances, are not to be treated as automata. There's trouble brooding.'

'Oh, if He only would be guided, so easily He might avoid a repetition of the former tragedy, and hold undisputed sway in the hearts of all men and women which the world contains.'

'I doubt the very easily; and anyhow, He won't be guided. I for one shall make no further attempt. I don't know what it is He proposes to Himself (I never could clearly understand what was the intention of the Christ of tradition), but I'm sure that it was something very different to what is in your mind. I am equally certain that the world has never seen, and will never suffer, such an autocrat as He suggests.'

'Jebb, I know you mean well, I know how you have devoted your whole life to the good of others, but I wish I could make you understand how every word you utter is a shock to my whole sense of decency and reverence.'

'Your sense of decency and reverence! You haven't any. You and Philipps and Robins, and all men of your kidney, have less of that sort of thing than I have. You are too familiar ever to be reverent.'

'Jebb, what noise is that?'

'He has gone out into the street. At sight of Him the people have started shouting. The police will have their hands full if they don't look out. Something very like the spirit of riot is abroad.'

'I must follow Him; I must try to keep close to Him, wherever He may go. Perhaps my assiduity may at last prevail. As it is, it all threatens to turn out so differently to what I had hoped.'

'Yes, you had hoped to be a prominent figure in the proceedings, but you are going to take no part in them at all; that's where the shoe pinches with you, Treadman.'

Mr. Treadman had not stayed to listen. He was already down the stairs and at the street door, to find that the Stranger had just passed through it, to be greeted by a chorus of exclamations from those who saw Him come.

The spacious roadway was filled with people from end to end—an eager, curious, excitable crowd. There were men, women, and children; but though it contained a sprinkling of persons of higher social rank, it was recruited mostly from that class which sees nothing objectionable in a crowd as such. Vehicular traffic was stopped. The police kept sufficient open space upon the pavement to permit of pedestrians passing to and fro. In front of the house was a surprising spectacle. Invalids of all sorts and kinds were there gathered together in heterogeneous assemblage. The officials, finding it impossible without using violence to prevent their appearance on the scene, had cleared a portion of the roadway for their accommodation, so that when He appeared, He found Himself confronted by all manner of sick. There were blind, lame, and dumb; idiots and misshapen folk; sufferers from all sorts of disease, in all stages of their maladies. Some were on the bed from which they were unable to raise themselves, some were on chairs, some on the bare ground. They had been brought from all parts of the city—young and old, male and female. There were those among them who had been there throughout the night.

When they saw Him come out of the door, those who could move at all began to press forward so that they might be able to reach Him, crying:

'Heal us! heal us!'

In their eagerness they bade fair to tread each other under foot; seeing which the officer who stood at the gate turned to Him, saying:

'Is it you these poor wretches have come to see? If you have encouraged them in their madness you have incurred a frightful responsibility; the deaths of many of them will be upon your head.'

He replied:

'Speak of that of which you have some understanding.' To the struggling, stricken crowd in front of Him He said: 'Go in peace and sin no more.'

Straightway they all were healed of their diseases. The sick sprang out of their beds and from off the ground, cripples threw away their crutches, the crooked were made straight, the blind could see, the dumb could talk. When they found that it was so they were beside themselves with joy. They laughed and sang, ran this way and that, giving vent to their feelings in divers strange fashions.

And all they that saw it were amazed, and presently they raised a great shout:

'It is Christ the King!'

They pressed forward to where He stood upon the step. Stretching out His hand, He held them back.

'Why do you call me king? Of what am I the king? Of your hearts and lives? Of your thoughts at your rising up and lying down? No. You know Me not. But because of this which you have seen you exclaim with your voice; your hearts are still. Who among you doeth My commandments? Is there one who has lived for Me? My name is on your tongues; your bodies you defile with all manner of evil. You esteem yourselves as gods. There are devils in hell who are nearer heaven than some of you. As was said to those of old, Except you be born again you know Me not. I know not you; call not upon My name. For service which is of the lips only is a thing hateful unto God.'

When He ceased to speak the people drew farther from Him and closer to each other, murmuring among themselves:

'Who is he? What are these things which he says? What have we done to him that he should speak to us like this?'

A great stillness came over the crowd; for, although they knew not why, they were ashamed.

When He came down into the street they made way for Him to pass, no one speaking as He went.

Chapter XVIII

The Young Man

The fame of these things passed from the frequenters of the streets and the hunters of notoriety to those in high places. The matter was discussed at a dinner which was given that night by a Secretary of State to certain dignitaries, both spiritual and temporal. There was no Mr. Treadman there. The atmosphere was sacrosanct. There was an absence of enthusiasm on any subject beneath the sun which, to minds of a certain order, is proper to sanctity. The conversation wandered from Shakespeare to the musical glasses; until at last something was said of the subject of the day.

It was the host who began. He was a person who had risen to his high position by a skilful manipulation of those methods which have made of politics a thing apart. A clever man, shrewd, versatile, desirous of being in the van of any movement which promised to achieve success.

'The evening papers are full of strange stories of what took place this morning at Maida Vale. They make one think.'

'I understand,' said Sir Robert Farquharson, known in the House of Commons as 'the Member for India,' 'that the people are quite excited. Indeed, one can see for oneself that there are an unusual number of people in the streets, and that they all seem talking of the same thing. It reminds one of the waves of religious frenzy which in India temporarily drive a whole city mad.'

'We don't go quite so far as that in London, fortunately. Still, the affair is odd. Either these things have been done, or they haven't. In either case, I confess myself puzzled.'

The Archbishop looked up from his plate.

'There seems to be nothing known about the person of any sort or kind—neither who he is, nor what he is, nor whence he comes. The most favourable supposition seems to be that he is mentally deranged.'

'Suppose he were the Christ?' The Archbishop looked down; his face wore a shocked expression. The Secretary smiled; he has not hesitated to let it be known that he is in bondage to no creed. 'That would indeed be to bring religion into the sphere of practical politics.'

'Not necessarily. It was a Roman blunder which placed it there before.'

This was the Earl of Hailsham, whose fame as a diplomatist is politically great.

'You think that Christ might come and go without any official notice being taken of the matter?'

'Certainly. Why not? That might, and would, have been the case before had Pontius Pilate been a wiser and a stronger man.'

'That point of view deserves consideration. Aren't you ignoring the fact that this is a Christian country?'

'In a social sense, Carruthers, most decidedly. I hope that we are all Christians in England—I know I am—because to be anything else would be the height of impropriety.'

The Secretary laughed outright.

'Your frankness shocks the Archbishop.'

Again the Archbishop looked up.

'I am not easily shocked at the difference of opinion on questions of taste. It is so easy to jeer at what others hold sacred.'

'My dear Archbishop, I do implore your pardon a thousand times; nothing was farther from my intention. I merely enunciated what I supposed to be a truism.'

'I am unfortunately aware, my lord, that Christianity is to some but a social form. But I believe, from my heart, that, relatively, they are few. I believe that to the great body of Englishmen and Englishwomen Christianity is still a vital force, probably more so today than it was some years ago. To the clergy I know it is; by their lives they prove it every hour of every day.'

'In a social or a spiritual sense? Because, as a vital force, it may act in either direction. Let me explain to you exactly what I mean. That it is nothing offensive you will see. My own Rector is a most estimable man; he, his curates, and his family are untiring in their efforts to increase the influence of the Church among the people. There is not a cottager in the parish who does not turn towards the Rectory in time of trouble—he would rather turn there than towards heaven. In that sense I say that the Rector's is a social, rather than a spiritual, influence; he himself would be the first to admit it. The work which the Church is doing in the East of London is social. The idea seems to be that if you improve the social conditions, spiritual improvement will follow. Does it? I wonder. Christianity is a vital force in a social sense, thank goodness! But my impression is that its followers await the Second Coming of their Founder with the same dilettante interest with which the Jews anticipate the rebuilding of Jerusalem. Both parties would be uncomfortably surprised if their anticipations were fulfilled. They would be confronted with a condition for which they were not in any way prepared. Candidly, wouldn't they? What would you yourself do if this person who is turning London topsy-turvy were actually the Christ?'

'I am unable to answer so very serious a question at a moment's notice.'

'In other words, you don't believe that he is the Christ; and nothing would make you believe. You know such things don't happen—if they ever did.'

'You would not believe even though one rose from the dead—eh, Archbishop?'

The question came from Sir William Braidwood, the surgeon. The Earl of Hailsham looked towards him down the table.

'By the way, what is the truth about that woman at the hospital?'

'The woman was dead; living, she was cancerous. He restored her to life; healed of her cancer. No greater miracle is recorded of the Christ of tradition. This afternoon a woman came to me who has been paralysed for nearly five years, unable to move hand or foot, to raise herself on her bed, or to do anything for herself whatever. She came on her own feet, ran up the stairs, radiant with life, health, and good spirits, in the full enjoyment of all her limbs. She was one of those who were at Maida Vale, whither she had been borne upon her bed. You should hear her account of what took place. The wonder to me is that the crowd was not driven stark, staring mad!'

'These things cause one to think furiously.' The Secretary sipped his wine. He addressed the Archbishop. 'Have you received any official intimation of what is taking place?'

'I have had letters, couched in the most extraordinary language, and even telegrams. Also verbal reports, full of the wildest and most contradictory statements. I occupy a position of extreme responsibility, in which my slightest word or action is liable to misconstruction.'

'Has it been clearly proved,' asked Farquharson, 'that he himself claims to be the Christ?' No one seemed to know; no one answered. 'Do I understand, Braidwood, that you are personally convinced that this person is possessed of supernatural powers?'

'I am; though it does not necessarily follow on that account that he is the Christ, any more than that he is Gautama Siddartha or Mahomet. I believe that we are all close to what is called the supernatural, that we are divided from it by something of no more definite texture than a membrane. We have only to break through that something to find such powers are. Possibly this person has performed that feat. My own impression is that he's a public danger.'

'A public danger? How?'

'Augustus Jebb called to see me before I came away—the social science man, I mean. He followed close on the heels of the woman of whom I told you. He was himself in Mrs. Powell's house at the time, and from a window saw all that occurred. He corroborates her story, with additions of his own. A few moments before he, with others, had an interview with the miracle-worker. He says that he was afraid of him, mentally, physically, morally, because of the possibilities which he saw in the man. He justifies his fear by two facts. As you are aware, this person stopped last night at the house of Mrs. Miriam Powell, the misguided creature who preaches what she calls social purity. She was a hale, hearty woman, in the prime of life, as late as yesterday afternoon. She was, however, a terrible bore. The probability is that, during the night, for some purpose of her own, she forced herself into her guest's presence; with the result that this morning she was a thing of horror.'

'In what sense?'

'Age had prematurely overtaken her—unnatural age. She looked and moved like a hag of ninety. She was mentally affected also, seeming haunted by an unceasing causeless terror. She kept repeating: "I have seen Him face to face!"—significant words. Jebb's other fact referred to Robins, the Salvation Army man. When Robins came into this person's presence he was attacked as with paralysis, and transformed into a nerveless coward. Jebb says that he is a pitiable object. His inference—which I am disposed to endorse—is, that if that person can do good he can also do evil, and that it is dependent upon his mood which he does. A man who can perform wholesale cures with a word may, for all we know, also strike down whole battalions with a word. His powers may be new to him, or the probability is that we should have heard of him before. As they become more familiar, to gratify a whim he may strike down a whole cityful. And there is another danger.'

'You pile up the agony, Braidwood.'

'Wait till I have finished. There are a number of wrong-headed persons who think that he may be used as a tool for their own purposes. For instance, Jebb actually endeavoured to induce him to transform London, as it were, with a touch of his wand.'

'What do you mean?'

'You know Jebb's panacea—better houses for the poor, and that sort of thing. He tried to persuade this person to provide the London poor with better houses, money in their pockets, clothes on their backs, and food in their stomachs, in the same instantaneous fashion in which he performed his miracle of healing.'

'Is Mr. Jebb mad?'

'I should say certainly not. He has been brought into contact with this person, and should be better able to judge of his powers than we are. He believes them to be limitless. Jebb himself was badly snubbed. But that is only the beginning. He tells me that the man Walters, the socialistic agitator, and his friends are determined to make a dead set at the wonder-worker, and to leave no stone unturned to induce him to bring about a revolution in London. The possibility of even such an attempt is not agreeable to contemplate.'

'If these things come to pass, religion—at least, so far as this gentleman is concerned—will at once be brought within the sphere of practical politics. Don't you think so, Hailsham?'

'It might bring something novel into the political arena. I should like to see how parties would divide upon such a question, and the shape which it would take. Would the question as to whether he was or was not the Christ be made the subject of a full-dress debate, and would the result of the ensuing division be accepted as final by everyone concerned?'

'I should say no. If the "ayes" had it in the House, the "noes" would have it in the country, and vice versâ.'

'Farquharson, you suggest some knowledge of English human nature. In our fortunate country obstinacy and contrariness are the dominant public notes. A Briton resents authority in matters of conscience, especially when it emanates from the ill-conditioned persons who occupy the benches in the Lords and Commons; which is why religious legislation is such a frightful failure.'

This with a sly glance at the Archbishop, who had been associated with a Bill for the Better Ordering of Public Worship.

The Duke of Trent joined in the conversation. He was a young man who had recently succeeded to the Dukedom. Coming from a cadet branch of the family, he had hitherto lived a life of comparative retirement. His present peers had not yet made up their minds as to the kind of character he was. He spoke with that little air of awkwardness peculiar to a certain sort of Englishman who approaches a serious subject. His first remark was addressed to Sir William Braidwood:

'But if this is the Christ, would you not expect Him to mete out justice as well as mercy? He may have come to condemn as well as to bless. In that case a sinner could hardly expect to force himself into His presence and escape unscathed.'

'On points of theology I refer you to the Archbishop. My point is, that an autocrat possessed of supernatural powers is a public danger.'

'Does that include God the Father? He is omnipotent. Whom He will He raises up, and whom He will He puts down. So we Christians believe.'

The Archbishop turned towards him.

'You are quite right, Duke; we know it. To suppose that Christ could be in any sense a public danger is not only blasphemous but absurd. Such a notion could only spring from something worse than ignorance. I take it that Sir William discredits the idea that about this person there is anything divine.'

'I believe He is the Christ!'

'You do?'

'I do.'

'But why?'

All eyes had turned towards the young man; who had gone white to the lips.

'I do not know that I am able to furnish you with what you would esteem a logical reason. Could the Apostles have given a mathematical demonstration of the causes of their belief? I only know that I feel Him in the air.'

'Of this room?'

'Yes, thank God! of this room.'

'You use strange words. Do you base your belief on his reported miracles?'

'Not entirely, though I entirely dissent from Sir William Braidwood's theory that we are near to what he calls the supernatural; except in the sense that we are near heaven, and that God is everywhere. Such works are only of Him. Man never wrought them; or never will. My mother loved Christ. She taught me to do so. Perhaps that is why I know that He is in London now.'

'What do you propose to do?'

'That is what troubles me. I don't know. I feel that I ought to do something, but—it is so stupid of me!—I don't know what.'

'Does your trouble resemble the rich young man's of whom some of us have read?'

This was the Earl of Hailsham. The Duke shook his head.

'No; it's not that. He knows that I will do anything I can do; but I don't think He wants me to do anything at all. He is content with the knowledge that I know He is here, that His presence makes me happy. I think that's it.'

Such sentiments from a young man were unusual. His hearers stared the more. The Archbishop said, gravely, sententiously:

'My dear Duke, I beg that you will give this matter your most serious consideration; that you will seek advice from those qualified to give it; and that only after the most careful deliberation you will say or do anything which you may afterwards regret. I confess I don't understand how you arrive at your conclusions. And I would point out to you very earnestly how much easier it is to do harm than good.'

The young man, leaning over on to the table, looked his senior curiously in the face.

'Don't you know that He is Christ—not in your heart of hearts?'

The question, and the tone of complete conviction with which it was put, seemed to cause the Archbishop some disturbance.

'My dear young friend, the hot blood of youth is in your veins; it makes you move faster than we old men. You are moved, I think, easily in this direction and in that, and are perhaps temperamentally disposed to take a good deal for granted.'

'I'm sorry you don't know. You yourself will be sorry afterwards.'

'After what?'

This again was Hailsham.

'After He has gone. He may not stay for long.'

'Trent, I find you a most interesting study. I won't do you the injustice to wonder if your attitude can be by any possibility a pose, but it takes a great deal for granted. For instance, it presumes that the legends found in what are called the four gospels are historical documents, which no man has believed yet.'

This roused the Archbishop.

'My lord, this is a monstrous assertion. It is to brand a great multitude of the world's best and greatest as liars—the whole host of the confessors!'

'They were the victims of self-delusion. There are degrees of belief. I have endeavoured to realise Christ as He is pictured in the gospels. I am sure no real believer of that Christ ever was a member of any church with which I am acquainted. That Christ is in ludicrous contrast with all that has been or is called Christianity.'

The Secretary interposed.

'Gently, Hailsham! How have we managed to wander into this discussion? If you are ready, gentlemen, we will go into the drawing-room. One or two ladies have promised to join us after dinner; I think we may find that some of them are already there. Archbishop, Hailsham will stultify himself by dragging religion into the sphere of practical politics yet.'

'I won't rest,' declared the Archbishop, as he rose from his chair, 'until I have seen this man.'

'Be careful how you commit yourself, and be sure that you are in good bodily health, and free from any sort of nervous trouble, before you go. Because, otherwise, it is quite within the range of possibility that you won't rest afterwards. And in any case you run a risk. My impression is that my suspicions will be verified before long, and that it will be seen only too plainly that this person is a grave public danger.'

This was Sir William Braidwood. Lord Hailsham exclaimed:

'That suggests something. What do you say, Trent, to our going tomorrow to pay our respects together?'

The Duke smiled.

'We should be odd associates. But I don't think that would matter. He knows that your opportunities have perhaps been small, and that your capacity is narrow. You might find a friend in Him after all. What a good thing it would be for you if you did!'

Hailsham laughed outright.

'Will you come?'

'I think not, until He calls me. I shall meet Him face to face in His own good time.'

Hailsham laid his hand upon the young man's shoulder.

'Do you know, I'm inclined to ask myself if I haven't chanced upon a Christian after all. I didn't know there was such a thing. But I'm beginning to wonder. If you really are a Christian after His pattern, you've the best of it. If I'm right, I gain nothing. But if you're right, what don't I lose?'

The young man said:

'He knows.'

PART III

THE PASSION OF THE PEOPLE

Chapter XIX

The Hunt and the Home

Wherever that day the Stranger went, He was observed of the people. It had been stated in a newspaper that a lame man seemed to be His invariable companion. The fact that such an one did limp at His side served as a mark of recognition; also the charcoal-burner, still in the attire in which he plied his forest trade, was an unusual figure in a London street. Mr. Treadman, issuing from the house at Maida Vale, had been unable to penetrate the crowd which closed behind them, so that his vociferous proclamations of identity were absent. Still, such a trio moving together through the London streets were hardly likely to escape observation.

Not that, for the most part, the Stranger's proceedings were marked by the unusual. He passed from street to street, looking at what was about Him, standing before the shops examining their contents, showing that sort of interest in His surroundings which denotes the visitor to town. Again and again He stopped to consider the passers-by, how they were as a continual stream.

'They are so many, and among them are so few!'

When He reached the top of Ludgate Hill, He looked up at St. Paul's Cathedral.

'This is a great house which men have builded. Let us go in.'

When they were in, He said:

'The Lord is not absent from this house. It is sweet to enter the place where they call upon His Name. If He were in their hearts, and not only on their tongues!'

A service was commencing. He joined the worshippers. There were many there that day who rejoiced exceedingly, although they knew not why.

When the service was over, and they were out in the street again, He said:

'It is good that the work of men's hands should be for the glory of God; yet if to build a house in His Name availed much, how full would the courts of heaven be. This He desires: a clean heart in a clean body; for where there is no sin He is. How does it profit a man to build unto God if he lives unto the world?'

When they came into Cheapside people were flocking into the restaurants for their mid-day meal. He said:

'Come, let us go with them; let us also eat.'

Entering, food was brought to them. The place was full. There was one man who, as he went out, spoke to the proprietor:

'That is the man of whom they are all talking. I know it. He frightens me.'

'He frightens you! What has he done?'

'It is not that he has done anything; it is that I dare not sit by him—I dare not. Let me go.'

'Are you sure that it is he?'

'I am very sure. Here is the money for what I have had—take it. Don't trouble about the change; only let me go.'

The speaker rushed into the street like one flying from the wrath to come.

There were those who had heard what he had said. Immediately it was whispered among them that He of whom such strange tales were told was in their very midst. Presently one said to the other:

'My daughter is dying of consumption; I wonder if he could do anything to cure her.'

A second said:

'My wife's sick of a fever. It might be worth my while to see if he could save further additions to my doctor's bill.'

A third:

'I've a cousin who's deformed—can't do anything for himself—a burden on all his friends. Now, if he could be made like the rest of us, what a good thing it would be for everyone concerned!'

A fourth:

'My father's suffering from some sort of brain disease. It's not enough to enable us to declare him legally insane, but it's more than sufficient to cause him to let his business go to rack and ruin. We don't know where it will end if the thing goes on. If this worker of wonders could do anything to make the dad the man he used to be!'

There were others who told similar tales. Soon they came to where He sat, each with his own petition. When he had heard them to an end, He said:

'You ask always; what is it you give?'

They were silent, for among them were not many givers. He said further:

'He among you who loves God, his prayer shall be answered.' Yet they were still. 'Is there not one who loves Him?'

One replied:

'Among those whom you healed this morning, how many were there who, as you call it, love God? Yet you healed them.

'Though I heal your bodies, your souls I cannot heal. As I said to them, I say to you: Go in peace, and sin no more.'

They went out guiltily, as men whose consciences troubled them. It was told up and down the street that He was there. So that when He came out a crowd was gathered at the door. Some of those who had petitioned Him had proclaimed that He had refused their requests; for so they had interpreted His words. When He appeared one cried in the crowd:

'Why didn't you heal them, like you did the others?'

And another:

'It seems easy enough, considering that you've only got to say a word.'

A third:

'Shame! Only a word, and he wouldn't say it.'

As if under the inspiration of some malign influence, the crowd, showing sudden temper, pressed upon Him. Someone shook his fist in His face, mocking Him:

'Go on! Go on back where you come from! We don't want you here!'

A big man forced his way through the people. When he had reached the Stranger's side he turned upon them in a rage.

'You blackguards, and worse than blackguards—you fools! What is it you think you are doing? This morning he healed a great crowd of things like you; you know it—you can't deny it. What does it matter who he is, or what he is? He has done you nothing but good, and in return what would you do to him? Shame upon you, shame!'

They fell back before the speaker's fiery words and the menace which was in his bearing. The Stranger said:

'Sir, your vehemence is great. You are not far from those that know Me.'

The big man replied:

'Whether I know you or whether I don't, I don't care to stand idly by when there are a hundred setting upon one. Besides, from all I hear, you've been doing great things for the sick and suffering, and the man who does that can always count upon me to lend him a hand. Though, mark my words, he who lays a crowd under an obligation is in danger. There is nothing to be feared so much as the gratitude of the many.'

Police appearing, the crowd in part dispersed. The Stranger began to make His way along the pavement, the big man at His side. Still, many of the people went with them, who being joined by others, frequently blocked the way. Locomotion becoming difficult, a police sergeant approached the Stranger.

'If you take my advice, sir, you'll get into a cab and drive off. We don't want to have any trouble with a lot like this, and I don't think we shall be able to stop them from following you without trouble.'

The big man said:

'Better do as the sergeant advises. Now that you have the reputation of working miracles, if you don't want to keep on reeling them off all day and all night too, you'd better take up your abode on the top of some inaccessible mountain, and conceal the fact that you are there. They'll make a raree-show of you if they can; and if they can't they'll perhaps turn ugly. Better let the sergeant call a cab—here are these idiots on to us again!'

He turned into the crowd.

'Let me go about My Father's business.'

They remained where they were, and let Him go.

But He had not gone far before He was perceived of others. It was told how He had performed another miracle by holding back the people at the Mansion House. Among the common sort there was at once a desire to see a further illustration of His powers. Throughout the afternoon they pressed upon Him more or less, sometimes fading away at the bidding of the police, sometimes swelling to an unwieldy throng. For the most part they pursued Him with shouts and cries.

'Do something—go on! Show us a miracle! Stop us from coming any further! Let's see how you do it!'

As the evening came He found Himself in a certain street in Islington where were private houses. The people pressed still closer; their cries grew louder, their importunity increasing because He gave them no heed. The police continually urged Him to call a cab and so escape. But He asked:

'Where shall I go? In what place shall I hide? How shall I do My Father's business if I seek a burrow beneath the ground?'

The constable replied:

'That's no affair of ours. You can see for yourself that this sort of thing can't be allowed to go on. If it does, I shouldn't be surprised if we had to look you up for your own protection. They'll do you a mischief if you don't look out.'

'What have I done to them, save healing those that were sick?'

'I'm not here to answer such questions. All I know is some queer ideas are getting about the town. If you knew anything about a London mob, you'd understand that the less you had to do with it the better.'

Someone called to the Stranger out of one of the little gardens which were in front of the houses.

'Come in here, sir, come in here! don't stand on ceremony; give those rascals the slip.' The speaker came down to the gate, shouting at the people. 'A lot of cowards I call you—yes, a lot of dirty cowards!

What has he done to you that you hound him about like this? Nothing, I'll be bound. If the police did their duty, they'd mow you down like grass.' He held the gate open. 'Come in, sir, come in! I can see by the look of you that you're an honest man; and it shan't be said that an honest man was chivied past George Kinloch's door by such scum as this without being offered shelter.'

The Stranger said:

'I thank you. I have here with Me two friends.'

'Bring them along with you; I can find room for three.'

The Stranger and His two disciples entered the gate. As they passed into the house the people groaned; there were cat-calls and cries of scorn. Mr. Kinloch, standing on his doorstep, shouted back at them:

'You clamouring curs! It is such creatures as you that disgrace humanity, and make one ashamed of being a man. Back to your kennels! herd with your kind! gloat on the offal that you love!' To the Stranger he exclaimed: 'I must apologise to you, sir, for the behaviour of these vagabonds. As a fellow-citizen of theirs, I feel I owe you an apology. I've no notion what you've done to offend them, but I'm pretty sure that the right is on your side.'

'I have done nothing, except heal some that were sick.'

'Heal some that were sick? Why, you don't mean to say—Are you he of whom all the world is talking? Ada! Nella! Lily!' The three whom he called came hastening. 'Here is he of whom we were speaking. It is he whom that swarm of riff-raff has been chivying. Bid him welcome! Sir, I am glad to have you for a guest, though only for a little.'

When He had washed and made ready He found them assembled in the best room of the house. The lamps were lit, the curtains drawn; within was peace. But through the window came the voices of the people in the street. Mr. Kinloch did his utmost to entertain his guest with conversation.

'These are my three daughters, as you have probably supposed. Their mother is dead.'

'I know their mother.'

'You knew her? Indeed! When and where? It must have been before she was married, because I don't seem to recognise your face.'

'I knew her before she was married, and after, and I know her now.'

'Now? My dear sir, she's dead!'

'Such as she do not die.'

Mr. Kinloch stared. The girl Ada touched him on the arm:

'Mother is in heaven; do you not understand?' She went with her sisters and stood before Him. 'It is so good to look upon Your face.'

'You have seen it from of old.'

'Then darkly, not as now, in the light.'

'Would that all the world saw Me in the light as you do! Then would My Father's brightness shine out upon all men, as does the sun. But yet they love the darkness rather than the light.'

Mr. Kinloch inquired, being puzzled:

'What is this? Have you met this gentleman before? Is he a friend of yours as well as of your mother's? I thought I knew something of all your acquaintance. I've always tried to make a rule of doing so. How comes it that you womenfolk have had a friend of whom I've been told nothing?'

Ada replied to his question with another.

'Father, do you not know Christ?'

'My dear girl, don't speak to me as if you were one of those women who go about with tracts in their hands! Haven't I always observed your mother's wishes, and seen that you went regularly to church? What do you mean by addressing your father as if he were a heathen?'

'This is Christ.'

'This? Girl, this is a man!'

'Father, have you forgotten that Christ was made man?'

'Yes, but that—that's some time ago.'

'He is made man again. Don't you understand?'

'No, I don't. Sir, I'm not what you might call very intellectual, and it's taken me all my time to find the means to bring these girls up as young women ought to be brought up. I suppose it's because I'm stupid, but, while I'll write myself down a Christian with any man, there's a lot of mystery about religion which is beyond my comprehension. There's a deal about you in the papers. I'm told you've been doing a wonderful amount of good to many who were beyond the reach of human help. For that I say, God bless you!'

The Stranger said: 'Amen.'

'At the same time there's much that is being said which I don't understand. I don't know who you are, or what you are, except that it's pretty clear to me that a man who has been doing what you have can't be very far from heaven; and if I ought to know, I'm sorry. God gave me a good wife, and she gave me three daughters who are like her. She's in heaven—I don't need anyone to tell me that; and if they'll only let her know, when they meet her among the angels, that I loved her while I'd breath, so long as she and they have all they want for ever and for ever, I don't care what God thinks it right to do with me. The end and aim of my life has been to make my wife and her children happy. If they're happy in heaven I'll be happy, too. That's a kind of happiness of which it will not be easy to deprive me, no matter where I am.'

'You are nearer to Me than you think.'

'Am I? We'll hope so. I like you; I like your looks; I like your voice; I like your ways; I like what you have brought into the house with you—it's a sort of a kind of peace. As Ada says—she knows; God tells that girl things which perhaps I'm too stupid to be told—it's good to look upon your face. Whatever happens in the time to come, I never shall be sorry that I've had a chance to see it.'

'You never shall.'

A voice louder than the rest was heard shouting in the street:

'Show us another miracle!'

Ada said:

'You hear that? Why, father, I do believe that a miracle is beginning to be worked in you!'

She smiled at him. He took her in his arms and kissed her.

Chapter XX

They that Would Ask with A Threat

There was a meeting of Universalists. This was a society whose meeting-place was in Soho. It called itself a club, using the word in a sense of its own, for anyone was admitted to its membership who chose to join; and, as a rule, all comers, whether members or not, were free to attend its meetings. It was a focus for discontent. To it came from all parts of the world the discontented, examples of that huge concourse which has a grudge against what is called Society—not of the silent part, which is in the majority, but of that militant section whose constant endeavour it is to goad the dumb into speech, in the hope and trust that the distance between speech and action will not be great.

The place was packed. There were women there as well as men—young and old—representatives of most of the nations which describe themselves as civilised; their common bond a common misery. The talk was old. But in the atmosphere that night was something new. Bellows had given vitality to the embers which smouldered in their hearts.

Henry Walters was speaking. They listened to him with a passionate eagerness which suggested how alluring was the dream which he proposed to wrest out of the arena of visions.

'I said to a policeman as I was coming in that I believed we were going to have our turn. He laughed. The police have had all the laughing. We'll laugh soon. We've been looking for a miracle, recognising that a miracle was the only thing that could help us. The arrival of a worker of miracles is a new factor in the situation with which the police, and all they represent, will have to reckon. It's just possible that they mayn't find him an easy reckoning. He who can raise a woman from the dead with a word can just as easily turn London upside down, and the police with it.

'We've heard of taking the kingdom of heaven by violence. I believe that it has been recommended by high authorities as a desirable method of procedure. I propose to try it. I propose we go tomorrow morning to this worker of miracles, saying: "You see how our wrongs ascend as a dense smoke unto Heaven. Put an end to them, so that they may cease to be an offence unto God." He has shown that he has bowels of compassion. I believe, if we put this plainly to him, with all the force that is in us, that the greatest of his miracles will be worked for us. If he will heal the sick, he will heal us; for we are sick unto more than death, since our pains have dragged us unto the gates of hell.

'The fashion of the healing we had better leave to him. Let us but point out that we come into the court of his justice asking for our rights; if he will give us what is ours we need not trouble about the manner of the giving. Let us but remind him that in the sight of God all men are equal; if he restores to us our equality, what does it matter how he does it? For the substance let the shadow go. But on so much we must insist; we must have the substance. We must be healed of our diseases, cured of our sores, relieved of our infirmities. If our just prayer is quickly heard, good. If not, the kingdom of heaven must be taken by violence, and shall be, if we are men and women. How are we profited, though miracles are worked for others, if none are worked for us? We stand most in need of the miraculous—none could come into this room, and see us, and deny it!—and we'll have it, or we'll know the reason why. He can scarcely smite us more heavily than we are already smitten. I wish to use no threats. I trust no one else will use them. I'm hopeful, since he has shown that he has sympathy for suffering, that he'll show sympathy for our sufferings. But—I say it not as a threat, but as a plain statement of a plain fact—if he won't do his best for us, we'll do our worst to him. God grant, however, that at last a Saviour has come to us in very deed!'

When Walters stopped a score of persons sprang to their feet. The chairman called upon a German, one Hans Küntz, wild, lean, unkempt, with something of frenzy in his air. He spoke English with a volubility which was only mastered by an occasional idiom; in a thin falsetto voice which was like a continuous shriek.

'I am hungry; that is not new. In the two small rooms where I live I have a wife and children who are also hungry; that also is not new. I run the risk of becoming more hungry by coming out to-night, and leaving work that must be finished by the morning. But when I hear that there is come to London one who can raise people from the dead, I say to my wife: "Then He can raise us too." My wife says: "Go and see." So to see I am come. With Mr. Walters I say, Let us all go and see—all, all that great London which when it works starves slowly, and when it does not work starves fast. We need not speak. We need but show Him our faces, how the skin but covers our bones. If he is not a devil, he will do to us what he has done to others: he will heal us and make us free. What I fear is that it is exaggerated what he has done—I have got beyond the region of hope. But if it is true, if but the half of it is true—if this morning he healed that crowd of people with a word, why should he not do the same to us? Why? Why? Did they deserve more than we? Are our needs not greater? We are the victims of others' sins. We are the slaves who sow, and reap, and garner, and yet are only suffered to eat the husks of the great stores of grain for which we give our lives. Surely this healer of the sick will give us a chance to live as men should live, and to die, when our time comes, as men should die! Oh, my brothers, if God has come among us He'll know! He'll know! And if He is a God of mercy, a God of love, and not a Siva, a destroyer, who delights in the groans and cries of bruised and broken hearts and lives, we have but to make to Him our petition, and He'll wipe the tears out of our eyes. To-night it is late, but in the morning, early, let us all go to Him—all! all!—all go!'

Out of the throng who were eager to speak next a woman was chosen—middle-aged, decently dressed, with fair hair and quiet eyes. Her voice was low, yet distinct, her manner calm, her language restrained, her bearing judicial rather than argumentative.

'Brothers Küntz and Walters seem to take it for granted that the God of the Christians is a God of love. I thought so when I was a child; I know better now. The idea seems to be supported in the present case by the fact that the person of whom we have heard so much has done works of healing, of mercy. It is not clear that, in all cases, to heal is to be merciful. Apart from that consideration, I would point out that the works in question have been spasmodic rather than continuous, the fruits, apparently, of momentary whims rather than of a settled policy. This afternoon his assistance was invited in similar cases. He declined. The crowd continually entreated him to do unto them as he had done unto others. Their requests were persistently ignored. It is plain, therefore, that one has not only to ask to receive. Nor is any attempt made to differentiate between the justice of contending claims. If this person is Divine, which I, personally, take leave to more than doubt, he is irresponsible. His actions are dependent on the mood of the moment.

'I am not saying this with any desire to throw cold water on the proposition which has been made to us. On the contrary, I think the suggestion that we should go to him in a body—as large a body as possible—and request his good offices on our behalf, an excellent one. At the same time, I cannot lose sight of one fact: that it is one thing to pray; to receive a satisfactory answer—or, indeed, an answer of any sort to one's prayer—is quite another. In our childish days we have prayed, believing, in vain. In the acuter agonies of our later years prayers have been wrung from us—always, still, in vain. There seems no adequate reason why, in the present case, we should pin our faith to the efficacy of prayer alone. The disease has always existed. Why should we suppose that the remedy has become accessible to whoever chooses to ask for it? If this person is Divine, he knows what we suffer; has always known, yet has done nothing. We are told that God is unchangeable, the same for ever and ever. The history of the world sustains this theory, inasmuch as it has always been replete with human suffering. That, therefore, disposes of any notion that it is at all likely that he has suddenly become sensitive to mere cries of pain.

'I would lay stress on one word which Brother Walters used more than once: violence. We are confronted with an opportunity which may never recur, and may vanish if not used quickly. Here is a person who has done remarkable things. The presumption is that he can do other remarkable things for us, if he chooses. He must be made to choose. That is the position.

'Let us clear our minds of cant. We are going to him with a good case. The reality of our grievances, the justice of our claims, he scarcely will be prepared to deny. Still, you will find him unwilling to do anything for us. Probably, assuming an air of Divine irresponsibility, he will decline to listen, or to discuss our case at all. Such is my own conviction. There will be a general rush for him tomorrow. All sorts and conditions of people will have an axe of their own to grind. In the confusion, ours will be easily and conveniently ignored. Therefore, I say, we must go in as large a body as possible, force him to give us an interview, compel him to accede to our request—that is, speak for us the same kind of word which he spoke for those sick people this morning. If he strikes us dead, he'll do himself no good and us no harm, for many of us would sooner be dead than as we are. Unless he does strike us dead we ought to stick to him until we have wrung from him our desire. It is possible that this is a case in which resolution may succeed. At the worst, in our plight, with everything to gain, and nothing—nothing—to lose, the attempt is one which is worth making, on the understanding that we will not take no for an answer, but will use all possible means to win a yes. We must make it as plain as it can be made that, if he will do nothing for us, he shall do nothing for others, at least on earth. What does it matter to us who enters heaven if the door is slammed in our faces?'

The next speaker was a man in corduroy trousers and a jacket and waistcoat which had once been whity-gray. He wore a cloth cap, and round his throat an old red handkerchief. His eyes moved uneasily in his head; when they were at rest they threatened. His face was clean-shaven, his voice husky. While he spoke, he kept his hands in his trousers pockets and his cap on his head. He plunged at once into the heart of what he had to say.

'I was one of them as shouted out this afternoon, "Show us a miracle!" And I was down at Maida Vale this morning, almost on top of them poor creatures as was more dead than alive. He just came out of the house, said two or three words, though what they was I couldn't catch, and there they was as right as if there'd never been nothing the matter with 'em, running about like you and me. And yet when I asked him to do something for me, though it'd have only cost him a word to do it—not he! He just walked on. I'm broke to the wide. Tuppence I've had since yesterday—not two bob this week. What I wanted was something to eat—just enough to keep me going till I'd a chance of a job. But though he done that this morning—and some queer ones there was among the crowd, I tell you!—he wouldn't pay attention to me, wouldn't even listen. What I want to know is, Why not? And that's what I mean to know before I've done.'

The sentiment met with approval. There were sympathetic murmurs. He was not the only hungry man in that audience.

'I'm in trouble—had the influenza, or whatever they call it, and lost my job. Never had one since. Jobs ain't easy found by blokes what seems dotty on their pins. My wife's in gaol—as honest a woman as ever lived; she'd have wore herself to the bone for me. Landlord wanted his rent; we hadn't a brown; I was down on my back; she didn't want me turned out into the street while I was like that, so she went and pawned some shirts what she'd got to iron. They gave her three months for it. She'd done two of 'em last Monday. Kid died last week and was buried by the parish. Gawd knows what she'll say when she hears of it when she comes out. Altogether I seem fairly off my level. So I say what the lady afore me says: Let's all go to him in the morning, and get him to understand how it is with us, and get him to say a word as'll do us good. And if he won't, why, as she says, we'll make him! That's all.'

There was no chance of choosing a successor from among the numerous volunteers. A man who seemed just insane enough to be dangerous chose himself. He broke into a vehement flood of objurgation, writhing and gesticulating as if desirous of working himself into a greater frenzy than he was in already. He had not been on his feet a minute before he had brought a large portion of his audience into a similar condition to himself.

'Make him, make him! That's the keynote. Share and share alike, that's our motto. No favouritism! The world stinks of favouritism; we'll have no more of it from him. We'll let him know it. What he does for one he must do for all. If he were to come into this room this minute, and were to help half of us, it would be the duty of all of us to go for him because he'd left the other half unhelped. He's been healing, has he? Who? Somebody. Not us. Why not us as well as them? He's got to give us what we want just as he gave them what they want, if we have to take him by the throat to take it out of him!'

'We will that!'

'Only got to say a word, has he, and the trick's done? Then he shall say that word for us, as he has for others, if we have to drag his tongue out by the roots to get at it!'

'That's it—that's the way to talk!'

'Work a miracle, can he, every time he opens his mouth? Then he shall work the miracles we want, or, by the living God, he shall never work another!'

The words were greeted with a chorus of approving shouts. The fellow screamed on. As his ravings grew worse, the excitement of his auditors waxed greater. Buffeted all their lives, as it seemed to them, by adverse winds, they were incapable of realising that they were in any way the victims of their own bad seamanship. For that incapacity, perhaps, they were not entirely to blame. They did not make themselves. That they should have been fashioned out of such poor materials was not the least of their misfortunes.

And their pains and griefs, humiliations and defeats, had been so various and so many that it was not strange that their wit had been abraded to the snapping-point; the more especially since it had been of such poor quality at first.

Chapter XXI

The Asking

In the morning the thoughts of England were turned towards that house in Islington: and no small number of its people were on their way to it. The newspapers besieged it with their representatives—on a useless quest, though their columns did not lack news on that account. Throughout the night the crowd increased in the street. The authorities began to be concerned. They acted as if the occasion of public interest was a fire. Placing a strong cordon of police at either end of the road, they made of it a private thoroughfare; only persons with what were empirically regarded as credentials were permitted to pass. Only after considerable hesitation was sickness allowed to be a passport. When it was officially decided to admit the physically suffering an extraordinary scene began to be enacted. It almost seemed as if all the hospitals and sick-rooms of London had been emptied of their occupants. They came in an unceasing stream. The police displayed their wonted skill in the management of the amazing crowd. Those who had been brought on beds were placed in the front ranks; those on chairs next; those who could stand, though only with the aid of crutches, at the back. The people had to be forced farther and farther away to make room for the sick that came; and yet before it was full day admission had to be refused to any more—every foot of available ground was occupied.

There were doctors present, some of whom were dissatisfied with the turn matters were taking. Perceiving, perhaps, that if it continued their occupation would be gone, they represented to the police that if certain of the sufferers did not receive immediate attention they might die. So that at an early hour their chief, Colonel Hardinge, who had just arrived, knocked at Mr. Kinloch's door. Ada opened.

'I understand that he whom these unfortunate people have come to see is at present in this house.'

'The Lord is in this house.'

'Quite so. We won't quarrel about description. The fact is, I'm told that if something isn't done for these poor creatures at once, they'll die. So, with your permission, I'll see the—er—person.'

'It is not with my permission, but with His. He is the Lord. When He wishes to see you, well. He does not wish to see you now.'

She shut the door in the Colonel's face.

'That's an abrupt young lady!'

This he said to the doctors and other persons who were standing at the gate. Among them was Sir William Braidwood, who replied:

'I don't know that she isn't right.'

'It's all very well for you to talk like that, but what am I to do? You tell me with one breath that if something isn't done people will die, and with another that because I try to get something done I merit a snubbing.'

'Exactly. This isn't a public institution; the girl has a right to resent your treating it as if it were. These people oughtn't to be here at all. Those who are responsible for some of them ought to be made to stand their trial for murder. This person, whoever he is, has promised nothing. They have not the slightest claim upon him. They are here as a pure speculation. Your men are to blame for allowing them to assemble in such a fashion, not the girl who endeavours to protect her guest from intrusion.'

Someone called out from the crowd:

'Ain't he coming, sir? I'm fair finished, I am—been here six hours. I'm clean done up.'

'What right have you to be there at all? You ought to be at home in bed.'

'I've come to be healed.'

'Come to be healed! I suppose if you want a hatful of money, you think you've only got to ask for it. You've no right to be here.'

Murmurs arose—cries, prayers, stifled execrations. An inspector said to his chief:

'If something isn't done, sir, I fancy there'll be trouble. Our men have difficulty in keeping order as it is. Half London must be here, and they're coming faster than ever. There's an ugly spirit about, and some ugly customers. If it becomes known that nothing is going to be done for these poor wretches, I don't know what will happen. How we are going to get them safely away is more than I can guess.'

'You hear what Sir William Braidwood says.'

'Begging Sir William's pardon, it's a choice of evils, and if I were you, sir, I should try again. They can't refuse to let you see this person. Not that I suppose he can do what they think he can, but still there you are.'

'He can do it.'

'With a word?'

'With a word.'

'Then he ought to.'

'Why? I can give you a thousand pounds with a word. But why ought I to?'

'That's different.'

'You'll find that a large number of people don't think it's different. These people want the gift of health; others in the crowd there want the gift of wealth. I dare wager there's no form of want which is not represented in that eager, greedy, lustful multitude. The excuse is common to them all: he can give it with a word. I am of your opinion, there will be trouble; because so many persons misunderstand the situation.'

Colonel Hardinge arrived at a decision:

'I think I will have another try. We can't have these people here all day, so if he won't have anything to do with them, the sooner they are cleared out of this, the better. What I have to do is to find out how it's going to be.'

He knocked again. This time the door was opened by Mr. Kinloch, who at once broke into voluble speech.

'It was you who came just now; what do you mean by coming again? What's the meaning of these outrageous proceedings? Can't I have a guest in my house without being subjected to this abominable nuisance?'

'I grant the nuisance, but would point out to you, sir, that we are the victims of it as well as you. If you will permit me to see your guest I will explain to him the position in a very few words. On his answer will depend our action.'

'My guest desires to be private; I must insist upon his privacy being respected. My daughter has been speaking to him. She tells me that he says that he has nothing to do with these people, and that they have nothing to do with him.'

'If that is the case, and that is really what he says, and I am to take it for an answer, then the matter is at an end.'

Ada's voice was heard at the back.

'Father, the Lord is coming.'

The Stranger came to the door. In a moment the Colonel's hat was in his hand.

'I beg a thousand pardons, sir, for what I cannot but feel is an intrusion; but the fact is, these foolish people have got it into their heads that they have only to ask you, and you will restore them to health. Am I to understand, and to give them to understand, that in so thinking they are under an entire delusion?'

'I will speak to them.'

The Stranger stood upon the doorstep. When they saw Him they began to press against each other, crying:

'Heal us! Heal us!'

'Why should I heal you?'

There was a momentary silence. Then someone said:

'Because you healed those others.'

'What they have you desire. It is so with you always. You cry to Me continually, Give! give! What is it you have given Me?'

The same voice replied:

'We have nothing to give.'

'You come to Me with a lie upon your lips.'

The fellow threw up his arms, crying:

'Lord! Lord! have mercy on me, Lord!'

He answered:

'Those among you that have given Me aught, though it is never so little, they shall be healed.' No one spoke or moved. 'Behold how many are the cheerful givers! I come not to give, but to receive. I seek My own, and find it not. All men desire something, offering nothing. This great city, knowing Me not, asks Me continually for what I have to give. Though I gave all it craves, it would be still farther off from heaven. It prizes not that which it has, but covets that which is another's, hating it because it is his. Return whence you came; cleanse your bodies; purify your hearts; think not always of yourselves; lift up your eyes; seek continually the knowledge of God. When you know Him but a thousandth part as He knows you, you need ask Him nothing, for He will give you all that you desire.'

With that He returned into the house.

When they saw Him go an outcry at once arose.

'Is that all? Only talk? Why, any parson could pitch a better yarn than that! Isn't He going to do anything? Isn't He going to heal us? What, not after healing those people yesterday at Maida Vale, and after our coming all this way and waiting all this time?'

The rougher sort who could use their limbs began to press forward towards the house, forcing down those who were weaker, many of whom filled the air with their cries and groans and curses. The police did their best to stem the confusion.

There came along the avenue on the pavement which the police had kept open Henry Walters and certain of his friends. They were escorted by a sergeant, who saluted Colonel Hardinge.

'This man Walters wants to see the person all the talk's about. There are a lot of his friends in the crowd, and rather than have any fuss I thought I'd let them come.'

'Right, sergeant. Mr. Walters is at liberty to see this person if this person is disposed to see him, which I'm rather inclined to doubt.'

'We'll see about that,' muttered Walters to his companions, as with them he hurried up the steps.

At the top he paused, regarding the poor wretches struggling fatuously in the street.

'That looks promising for us. So he won't heal them. Why? No reason given, I suppose. I dare say he won't heal us; for the same reason. Well, we'll see. Mind you shut the front door when we go in. I rather fancy we shall want some persuasion before we see the logic of such a reason as that.'

The door was closed as he suggested. In the hall he was met by Ada.

'What is it that you want?'

'You know very well what it is. We want a few words with the stranger who is in this house.'

'It is the Lord!'

'Very well. We want a few words with the Lord.'

'You cannot enter His presence uninvited.'

'Can't we? I think you are mistaken. Is He in that room? Stand aside and let me see.'

'You may not pass.'

'Don't be silly. We're in no mood for manners. Will you move, or must I make you? Do you hear? Come away.'

He laid his hand upon the girl's shoulder. As he did so the Stranger stood in the open door. When they saw Him, and perceived how in silence He regarded them, they drew a little back, as if perplexed. Then Walters spoke:

'I'm told that you are Christ.'

'What has Christ to do with you, or you with Christ?'

'That's not an answer to my question. However, without entering into the question of who you are, it seems that you can work wonders when you choose.'

There was a pause as if for a reply. The Stranger was still, so Walters went on.

'We represent a number of persons who are as the sands of the sea for multitude, the victims of man's injustice and of God's.'

'With God there is no injustice.'

'That is your opinion. We won't argue the point; it's not ours. We come to plead the cause of myriads of people who have never known happiness from the day they were born. Some of them toil early and late for a beggarly wage; many of them are denied the opportunity of even doing that. They have tried every legitimate means of bettering their condition. They have hoped long, striven often, always to be baffled. Their brother men press them back into the mire, and tread them down in it. We suggest that their case is worthy your consideration. Their plight is worse today than it ever was; they lack everything. Health some of them never had; they came into the world under conditions which rendered it impossible. Most of them who had it have lost it long ago. Society compels them to live lives in which health is a thing unknown. Their courage has been sapped by continuous failure. Hope is dead. Joy they never knew. Misery is their one possession. Under these circumstances you will perceive that if you desire to do something for them it will not be difficult to find something which should be done.'

Another pause; still no reply.

'We do not wish to cumber you with suggestions; we only ask you to do something. It will be plain to your sense of justice that there could be no fitter subjects for benevolence. Yet all that we request of you is to be just. You are showering gifts broadcast. Be just; give also something to them to whom nothing ever has been given. I have the pleasure to await your answer.'

He answered nothing.

'What are we to understand by your silence?—that you lack the power, or the will? We ask you, with all possible courtesy, for an answer. Courtesy useless? Still nothing? There is a limit even to our civility. Understand, also, that we mean to have an answer—somehow.'

Ada touched him on the arm, whispering:

'It is the Lord!'

'Is he a friend of yours?'

'He is a Friend of all the world.'

'It doesn't look like it at present, though we hope to find it the case before we've finished. Come, sir! You hear what this young lady says of you. We're waiting to hear how you propose to show that you're a friend of that great host of suffering souls on whose behalf we've come to plead to you.'

Yet He was still. Walters turned to his associates.

'You see how it is? It's as I expected, as was foreseen last night. If we want anything, we've got to take the kingdom of heaven by violence. Are we going to take it, or are we going to sneak away with our tails between our legs?'

The woman answered who had spoken at the meeting the night before—the fair-haired woman, with the soft voice and quiet eyes:

'We are going to take it.' She went close to the Stranger. 'Answer the question which has been put to you.' When He continued silent, she struck Him on the cheek with her open palm, saying: 'Coward!'

Ada came rushing forward with her father and her sisters. With a movement of His hand He kept them back. Walters applauded the woman's action.

'That's right—for a beginning; but he'll want more than that. Let me talk to him.' He occupied the woman's place. 'We've nothing to lose. You may strike us dead; we may as well be dead as living the sort of life with which we are familiar; it is a living death. I defy you to cast us into a worse hell than that in which we move all day and every day. If you are Christ, you have a chance of winning more adherents than were ever won for you by all the preaching through all the ages, and with a few words. If you are man, we will make you king over all the earth, and all the world will cry with one heart and one voice: "God save the King!" And whether you are Christ or man, every heart will be filled with your praises, and night and morning old and young will call with blessings on your name. Is not that a prospect pleasing even unto God? And all this for the utterance of perhaps a dozen words. That is one side of the shield. Does it not commend itself to you? I ask you for an answer.

'None? Still dumb? I'll show you something of the other side. If you are resolute to shut your ears to our cries, and your eyes to our misery, we'll crucify you again. Don't think that those police outside will help you, or anything of that sort, because you'll be nursing a delusion. You'll be crucified by a world in arms. When it is known that with a word you can dry the tears that are in men's eyes, and yet refuse to utter it—when that is generally known, it will be sufficient. For it will have been clearly demonstrated that you must be a monster of whom the world must be rid at all and any cost. Given such a capacity, none but a monster would refuse to exercise it. And the fact that, according to some narrow code of scholastic reasoning, you may be a faultless monster will make the fact worse, not better. For faultlessness of that sort is in continual, cruel, crushing opposition to poor, weak, human nature. Now will you give me an answer?'

When none came, and His glance continued fixed upon the other's face with a strange, unfaltering intensity, Walters went still closer.

'Shall I shake the answer out of you?' Putting up his hand, he took the Stranger by the throat; and when He offered no resistance, began to shake Him to and fro. Ada, running forward, struck at Walters with so much force that, taken by surprise, he let the Stranger go. She cried:

'It is the Lord! It is the Lord!'

'What is that to us? Why doesn't he speak when he's spoken to? Is he a wooden block? You take care what you do, my girl. You'd be better employed in inducing your friend to answer us. Lord or no Lord. There'd be no trouble if he'd treat us like creatures of flesh and blood. If he'd a spark of feeling in his breast, he'd recognise that the very pitifulness of our condition—our misery, our despair!—entitles us to something more than the brand of his scornful silence; he'd at least answer yes or no unto our prayers.'

Ada wept as if her heart would break, sobbing out from amidst her grief:

'It is the Christ! It is the Lord Christ!'

Her father, forcing his way to the front door, had summoned assistance. A burly sergeant came marching in.

'What's the matter here? Oh, Mr. Walters, it's you! You're not wanted in here. Out you go—all of you. If you take my advice you'll go home, and you'll get your friends to go home too. There'll be some trouble if you don't take care!'

'Go home? Sergeant, you see that Man? Have you anywhere a tender place? Is there any little thing which, if you had it, would make your life brighter and more worth the living? That Man, by the utterance of a word, can make of your life one long, glad song; give you everything you are righteously entitled to deserve; so they tell me. Go home to the kennels in which we herd when the Christ who has come to release us from our bondage will not move a finger, or do aught to loose our bonds, but, seeing how we writhe in them, stands mutely by? No, sergeant. We'll not go home till we've had a reckoning with Him.'

He stretched out his arm, pointing at the Stranger.

'I'll meet you at another Calvary. You've crucified me and mine through the ages, and would crucify us still, finding it a royal sport at which it were blasphemy to cavil. Beware lest, in return, you yourself are not crucified again.'

When Walters and his associates had gone, the sergeant said, addressing the Stranger:

'I'm only doing my duty in telling you that the sooner you clear out of this, the better it'll be for everyone concerned. You're getting yourself disliked in a way which may turn out nasty for you, in spite of anything we can do. There's half a dozen people dead out in the street because of you, and there's worse to come, so take my tip and get out the back way somewhere. Find a new address, and when you have found it keep it to yourself. We don't want to have London turned upside down for anyone, no matter who it is.'

The sergeant went. And then words came from the Stranger's lips, as if they had been wrung from His heart; for the sweat stood on His brow:

'Father, is it, then, for this that I am come to the children that call upon My Name in this great city, where on every hand are churches built for men to worship Christ? What is this idol which they have fashioned, calling it after My Name, so that wherever I go I find a Christ which is not Me? Lord! Lord! they cry; and when the Lord comes they say, It is not you we called, but another. They deny Me to My face. The things I would they know not. In their blindness, knowing nothing, they would be gods unto themselves, making of You a plaything, the servant of their wills. As of old, they know not what they do. Aforetime, by God's chosen people was I nailed unto a tree. Am I again to suffer shame at the hands of those that call themselves My children? Yet, Father, let it be so if it is Your will.'

Chapter XXII

A Seminary Priest

In the street was riot; confusion which momentarily threatened to become worse confounded. In the press were dignitaries of the Church; that Archbishop whom we met at dinner; Cardinal De Vere, whose grace of bearing ornaments the Roman establishment in England; with him a young seminary priest, one Father Nevill. The two high clerics were on a common errand. Their carriages encountering each other on the outskirts of the crowd, they had accepted the services of a friendly constable, who offered to pilot them through the excited people. At his heels they came, scarcely in the ecclesiastical state which their dignity desired.

As they neared the house they were met by the departing Mr. Walters and his friends. Recognising who they were, Walters stopped to shout at them in his stentorian tones:

'So the High Priests have come! To do reverence to their Master? To prostrate themselves at His feet in the dust, or to play the patron? To you, perhaps, He'll condescend; with these who, in their misery, trample each other under foot He'll have no commerce; has not even a word with which to answer them. But you, Archbishop and Cardinal, Princes of His Most Holy Church, perhaps He'll have a hand for each of you. For to those that have shall be given, and from those that have not shall be taken away. He'll hardly do violence to that most excellent Christian doctrine. Tell Him how much you have that should be other men's; maybe He'll strip them of their skins to give you more.'

The constable thrust him aside.

'Move on, there! move on! That's enough of that nonsense!'

'Oh yes,' said Walters, as they forced him back into the seething throng; 'oh yes, one soon has enough of nonsense of that kind. Christ has come! God help us all!'

On the steps that led up to the door a woman fought with the police. She was as a mad thing, screaming in her agony:

'Let me see Christ! Let me see Him! My daughter's dead! I brought her to be healed; she's been killed in the crowd; I want Him to bring her back to life. Let me see Christ! Let me see Him!'

They would not. Lifting her off her feet, they bore her back among the people.

'What a terrible scene!' murmured the Archbishop. 'What lamentable and dangerous excitement!'

'You represent a Church, my dear Archbishop,' replied the Cardinal, 'which advocates the freedom of private judgment. These proceedings suggest that your advocacy may have met with even undesired success.'

The Archbishop, looking about him with dubious glances, said to the policeman who had constituted himself their guide:

'This sort of thing almost makes one physically anxious. The people seem to be half beside themselves.'

'You may well say that, my lord. I never saw a crowd in such a mood before; and I've seen a few. I hear they've sent for the soldiers.'

'The soldiers? Dear, dear! how infinitely sad!'

When they were seen on the steps, guarded by the police, waiting for the door to open, the crowd yelled at them. The Archbishop observed to his companion:

'I'm not sure, after all, that it was wise of me to come. Sometimes it is not easy to know what to do for the best. I certainly did not expect to find myself in the midst of such a scene of popular frenzy.'

Said the Cardinal:

'It at least enables us to see one phase of Protestant England.'

They were admitted by Ada, to whom the Archbishop introduced himself.

'I am the Archbishop, and this is Cardinal De Vere. We have come to see the person who is the cause of all this turmoil.'

Ada stopped before the open door of a room.

'This is the Lord!'

Within stood the Stranger, as one who listens to that which he desires, yet fears he will not hear: who looks for that for which he yearns, yet knows he will not see. The Archbishop fitted his glasses on his nose.

'Is this the person? Really! How very interesting! You don't say so!'

Since the Stranger had paid no heed to their advent, the Archbishop addressed himself to Him courteously:

'Pardon me if this seems an intrusion, or if I have come at an inconvenient moment, but I have received such extraordinary accounts of your proceedings that, as head of the English Church, I felt bound to take them, to some extent, under my official cognisance.'

The Stranger, looking at him, inquired:

'In your churches whom do you worship?'

'My dear sir! What an extraordinary question!'

'What idol have you fashioned which you call after My Name?'

'Idol! Really, really!'

'Why do you cry continually: "Come quickly!" when you would not I should come?'

'What very peculiar questions, betraying a complete ignorance of the merest rudiments of common knowledge! Is it possible that you are unaware that I am the head of the Christian hierarchy?'

Said the Cardinal:

'Of the English branch of the Protestant hierarchy, I think, Archbishop, you should rather put it. You are hardly the undisputed head of even that. Do your Nonconformist friends admit your primacy? They form a not inconsiderable section of English Protestantism. When informing ignorance let us endeavour to be accurate.'

'The differences are not essential. We are all branches of one tree, whose stem is Christ. To return to the point. This is hardly a moment, Cardinal, for theological niceties.'

'You were tendering information; I merely wished it to be correct, for which I must ask you to forgive me.'

'Your Eminence is ironical. However, as I said, to return to the point. The public mind appears to be in a state of most lamentable excitement. The exact cause I do not pretend to understand. But if your intentions are what I hope they are, you can scarcely fail to perceive that you owe it to yourself to remedy a condition of affairs which already promises to be serious. I am told that there is a notion abroad that you have advanced pretensions which I am almost convinced you have not done. I wish you to inform me, and to give me authority to inform the public, who and what you are, and what is the purport of your presence here.'

'I am He that you know not of.'

'That, my dear sir, is the very point. I am advised that you are possessed of some singular powers. I wish to know who the person is who has these powers, and how he comes to have them.'

'There is one of you that knows.'

The young priest advanced, saying:

'I know You, Lord!'

The Stranger held out to him His hand.

'Welcome, friend!'

'My Lord and my Master!'

While they still stood hand in hand, the Stranger said:

'There are those that know Me, nor are they few. Yet what are they among so many? In all the far places of the world men call upon My Name, yet know so little of what is in their hearts that they would destroy Me for being He to whom they call.'

'But shall the day never come when they shall know You?'

'Of themselves they must find Me out. Not by a miracle shall a man be brought unto the knowledge of God.'

Cardinal De Vere said to the young priest:

'Your stock of information appears to be greater than that of your spiritual superiors, Father. At Louvain do they teach such forwardness, or is this an acquaintance of your seminary days?'

'Yes, Eminence, indeed, and of before them too. For this is our Lord and Saviour Jesus Christ, who died for us, yet lives again, to whose service I have dedicated my life, and your Eminence your life also.'

'My son, let not your tongue betray you into speaking folly. For shame, my son, for shame!'

'But does not your Eminence know this is the Lord? Can you look upon His face and not see that it is He, or enter into His presence and not know that He is here?'

'Put a bridle upon that insolent tongue of yours. Come from that dangerous fellow.'

'Fellow? Eminence, it is the Lord! It is the Lord!' He turned to the Stranger. 'Lord Jesus, open the eyes of his Eminence, that he may see You, and his heart, that he may know that You are here!'

'Did I not say that no miracle shall bring a man to the knowledge of Me? If of himself he knows Me not, he will not know Me though I raise him out of hell to heaven.'

The young priest turned again to the Cardinal.

'But, Eminence, it is so strange! so wonderful! Your vocation is for Christ; you point always to His cross; you keep your eyes upon His face; and yet—and yet you do not know Him now that He is here! Oh, it is past believing! and you, sir, you are also a religious. Surely you know this is the Lord?'

This was to the Archbishop, who began to stammer:

'I—I know, my dear young friend, that you—you are saying some very extraordinary things—things which you—you ought to carefully consider before you—you utter them. Especially when I consider your—your almost tender years.'

'Extraordinary things! It is the Lord! it is the Lord! How shall you wonder at those who denied Him at the first if you, who preach Him, deny Him now? Oh, Eminence! oh, sir! look and see. It is the Lord!'

'Silence, sir! Another word of the sort and you are excommunicated.'

'For knowing it is the Lord?'

'For one thing, sir—for not knowing that on such matters Holy Church pronounces. Did they teach you so badly at Louvain that you have still to learn that in the presence of authority it is the business of a little seminary priest to preserve a reverent silence? It is not for you to oppose your variations of the creed upon your spiritual superiors, but to receive, with a discreet meekness, and in silence, your articles of faith from them.'

'If the Lord proclaims Himself, are His children to refuse Him recognition until the Church commands?'

'You had better return to your seminary, my son—and shall—to receive instruction in the rudiments of the Catholic faith.'

'If for any cause the Church withholds its command, is the Lord to depart unrecognised?'

'Say nothing further, sir, till you have been with your confessor. I command you to be silent until then.'

'Is, then, the Church against the Lord? It cannot be—it cannot be!' The young priest turned to the Stranger with on his face surprise, fear, wonder. 'Lord, of those that are here are You known to me alone?'

Ada came forward with her sisters.

'We also know the Lord.'

The Stranger said:

'Is it not written that many are called, but few chosen? As it was, is now, and ever will be. It is well that you know Me, and these that are the daughters of one who knows Me as I would be known; and there are those that know Me nearly.' With that He looked at Mr. Kinloch. 'Also here and there among the multitudes whom God has fashioned in His own image am I known, and in the hidden places of the world. Where quiet is, there am I often. Men that strive with their fellows in the midst of the tumult for the seats of the mighty call much upon My Name, but have Me little in their hearts; there is not room. Those that make but little noise, but are content with the lower seats, waiting upon My Father's will, they have Me much in their hearts, for there is room. Wherefore I beseech you to continue a little priest in a seminary, great in the knowledge of My Father, rather than a pillar of the Church, holding up heaven on your hands: for he that seeks to bear up heaven is of a surety cast down into hell. Would, then, that all men might be little men, since in My Father's presence they might have a better chance of standing high.'

The Cardinal, holding himself very straight, went closer to the young priest. His voice was stern.

'Father Nevill, your parents were my friends; because of that I have attached you to my person; because, also, of that I am unwilling to see you put yourself outside the pale of Holy Church as becomes a fool rather than a man of sense. What hallucination blinds you I cannot say. Your condition is probably one which calls for a medical diagnosis rather than for mine. How you can be the even momentary victim of so poor an impostor is beyond my understanding. But it ill becomes such as I am to seek for explanations from such as you. Your part is to obey, and only to obey. Therefore I bid you instantly to leave this—fellow; bow your head, and seek with shame absolution for your grievous sin. Do this at once, or it will be too late.'

When the young priest was about to reply, the Stranger, going to the Cardinal, looking him in the face, asked: 'Am I an impostor?'

The Cardinal did his best to meet His look, and return Him glance for glance. Presently his eyes faltered; he looked down. His lips twitched as if to speak. His gaze returned to the Stranger's countenance. But only for a moment. Suddenly he put up his hands before his face as if to shield it from the impact of the pain and sorrow which were in His eyes. He muttered:

'What have I to do with you?'

'Nothing; verily, and alas!'

'Why have you come to judge me before my time?'

'Your time comes soon.'

The Cardinal, dropping his hands, straightened himself again, as if endeavouring to get another grip upon his courage.

'I lean on Holy Church. She will sustain me.'

'Against Me?'

The Cardinal staggered against the wall, trembling so that he could hardly stand. The Archbishop cried, also trembling:

'What ails your Eminence? Cardinal, what is wrong?'

His Eminence replied, as if he all at once were short of breath:

'The rock—on which—the Church is founded—slips beneath my feet!'

The Archbishop surveyed him with frightened eyes.

Chapter XXIII

And the Child

The noise in the street had continued without ceasing. It grew louder. A sound arose as of many voices shrieking. While it still filled the air the lame man and the charcoal-burner descended from an upper room. They spoke of the tumult.

'The people are fighting with the police as if they have gone mad.'

'They seek Me,' said the Stranger.

The lame man looked at him anxiously.

'You!'

'Even Me. Fear not. All will be well.'

'Who are these persons?' inquired the Archbishop.

'They are of those that know Me.'

'Ay,' said the charcoal-burner, 'I know You—know You very well, I do. So did my old woman; she knowed You, too. I be that glad to have seen You. It's done me real good, that it have.'

'You have been with me so long; then this little while, and soon for ever.'

'Ay, very soon.'

'Father, these are of those that know Thy Son.'

He touched with His hand the six persons that were about Him.

The Archbishop plucked the Cardinal by the sleeve.

'I—I really think we'd better go. I—I'm not feeling very well.'

There came a succession of crashes. The Cardinal stood up.

'What's that? It's stones against the windows. Unless I err, they have shivered every pane.'

Someone knocked loudly at the door. The Cardinal moved as if to open. The Archbishop sought to restrain him.

'What are you doing? It isn't safe to open. The people may come in.'

The Cardinal smiled.

'Let them. The sooner the thing is done the better. To you and me what does it matter what comes?'

On the doorstep stood that Secretary of State who had given the dinner at which the Archbishop had been present. Behind him was the yelling mob.

'Your Eminence! This is an unexpected pleasure. The Archbishop, too! How delightful! The people seem in a curious frame of mind; our friend Braidwood is justified—already. It's a wonder I'm here alive. I am told that several persons have been killed in the crowd—terrible! terrible! My own opinion is that we're threatened with the most serious riot which London has known in my time. Ah, dear sir!' He bowed to the Stranger. 'I need not ask if you are he to whom I desire to tender my sincerest salutations. There is that about you which tells me that I stand in the presence of no mean person. Unfortunately, I am so constituted as to be incapable of those more ardent feelings which are to the enthusiast his indispensable equipment. Therefore I am not of that material out of which they fashion devotees. Yet, since I cannot doubt that my trifling personal peculiarities are known to him who, as I am informed, knows all, I venture to trust that they will be regarded as extenuating circumstances should I ever stand in instant need of palliation.'

The Stranger was still.

The stones still rattled against the windows, smashed against the door. Again there came a knocking. The tumult had grown so great, the cries so threatening, that those within were trembling, hesitating what to do. When the Stranger moved towards the door, the Secretary of State prevented Him.

'Sir, I beg of you! I fear it is you they wish to see, with what purpose you may imagine from the noise which they are making. Permit me to answer the knocking. At the present moment I am of less public interest than you.'

He opened. There was an excited sergeant of police.

'The person who's in here must get away by the back somewhere at once; those are my orders. The people have found out that they can get to this house from the street behind; they're starting off to do it. We don't want murder done, and there will be murder if he doesn't take himself off pretty quick.'

'Is it so bad as that?'

'So bad as that? Look at them yourself. I never saw them in such a state. They're stark, staring mad. All the streets about are full of them; they're all the same. That man Walters and his friends have been working a lot of them into a frenzy; murder is what they mean. Then there's over a hundred been killed in front here, so I'm told—poor wretches who came to be healed. The crowd will tear him to pieces if they get him. He must get away somehow over the walls at the back.'

'Over the walls at the back?'

'He can't get away by the front. We couldn't save him—nobody could. I tell you they'll tear him to pieces.'

As the sergeant spoke the Stranger came and stood at the door by the Secretary of State. A policeman rushed up the steps bearing something in his arms. He addressed the sergeant.

'This child's dead. Sir William Braidwood says most of the bones in its body are broken; it's crushed nearly to a jelly. It doesn't seem to have had any friends or anything. Could you see it taken into the house?'

The sergeant received the child. The Stranger said to him: 'Give it to Me.'

'You? Why you? Let it be taken into the house and put decent.'

'Give Me the child.'

He took the child and pressed it to His bosom, and the child, opening its eyes, looked up at Him. He kissed it on the brow.

'You have been asleep,' He said.

The child sat up in His arms and laughed.

The Archbishop whispered to the Cardinal:

'The child lives!'

The Stranger cried to those that were within the house:

'I return whence I came. Come there to Me.'

And a great hush fell on all the people, so that on a sudden they were still. And they fell back, so that a lane was formed in their midst, along which He went, with the child, laughing, in His arms.

It was as if the people had been carved out of stone. They moved neither limb nor feature, nor seemed to breathe, but stayed in the uncouth attitudes in which they had been flung by passion, with their faces as rage had distorted them, their mouths open as they had vomited blasphemies, their eyes glaring, their fists clenched.

Through the stricken people in the silent streets the Stranger went, the child laughing in His arms—on and on, on and on. Whither He went, no man knew. Nor has He been seen of any since, nor the child either.

And when He had gone, a great sigh went over all the people. Behold, they wept!

Richard Marsh – A Short Biography

Richard Bernard Heldmann was born on 12th October 1857, in St Johns Wood, North London, to parents Joseph Heldmann and Emma Marsh.

Shortly after his birth his father became ensnared in a bankruptcy proceedings which enforced the abandonment of a career as a merchant for that of a schoolmaster at a school in Hammersmith, West London.

By his early 20's the young Heldmann, showing a talent for writing, began publishing fiction. In 1880, he began to publish works of boys' school and adventure stories for the myriad magazine publications all eager for good well-written content. The most important of these was Union Jack, one of the better quality boys' weekly magazine associated with the popular authors G. A. Henty and W.H.G. Kingston.

Heldmann was promoted to co-editor in October 1882, but his association with the publication ended suddenly in June 1883. After this, Heldmann published no further fiction under that name.

The reason at the time was not immediately apparent but in April 1884 Heldmann was sentenced to 18 months of hard labour for issuing a series of cheques, all forged, in France and Britain the year before.

In order to be well away from the scandal and damage this had caused to his reputation Heldmann adopted a pseudonym on his release from jail. Shortly thereafter the name 'Richard Marsh' began to appear in the literary periodicals. The use of his mother's maiden name seems both a release from the criminal record now associated with his given name and a lifeline to a fresh beginning.

A stroke of very good fortune arrived when his novel The Beetle was published in 1897. There had been more than a few previous publications of his works but The Beetle would turn out to be his greatest commercial success and added some much-needed gravitas to his literary reputation. The story concerns a mysterious oriental person who follows a British politician to London, and then wreaks havoc with his powers of hypnosis and shape-shifting. The Beetle has some similar aspects to certain other novels of the period, including those such as Bram Stoker's Dracula, George du Maurier's Trilby, and Sax Rohmer's many Fu Manchu novels. Like Dracula, and also the sensation novels written by Wilkie Collins and others during the 1860s, The Beetle is narrated from the various viewpoints of multiple characters to create suspense. The novel is also layered with many themes and issues of the Victorian era including women's rights, unemployment, urban poverty, radical politics, homosexuality, science, and Britain's imperial adventures, particularly in regard to Egypt and the Sudan. The Beetle sold out upon its initial print run and thereafter sold well for the next several decades. After Marsh's early death the novel's story was made into a film and adapted for the London stage, both in the 1920's.

It should also be noted that in the year of its first publication it outsold Dracula, then also in its first year of publication. In hindsight a remarkable achievement.

Marsh was a prolific writer and wrote almost 80 volumes of fiction as well as many short stories, across several genres from horror and crime to romance and humour.

However, at horror he was particularly adept. Works such as The Goddess: A Demon (1900), in which an Indian sacrificial idol comes to life with murderous resolve, and The Joss: A Reversion (1901), whose central premise is that of an Englishman who transforms himself into a hideous oriental idol are prime examples.

An important element of many of Marsh's novels is the investigation of the mystery. Several of his novels are centered on the crime and its subsequent detection. In the novel Philip Bennion's Death

(1897) a bachelor is discovered dead the day after discussing Thomas De Quincey's essay on murder as a fine art, and his neighbour and friend begin efforts to solve his death. In The Datchet Diamonds (1898) a young man who has lost a fortune on the stock market mistakenly swaps bags with a diamond thief, and then find himself pursued by both the thieves and police. In A Spoiler of Men (1905), Marsh puts together crime and science-fiction; the gentleman-criminal villain renders people slaves to his will by a chemical injection.

As with many authors success with popular fiction was never quite enough. He also wanted to be regarded as a serious author. His novel A Second Coming (1900) imagines Christ's return to an early-20th century London and is his most well-handled attempt in that pursuit.

His prolific output of short stories ensured his being published in a plethora of magazines including Household Words, Cornhill Magazine, The Strand Magazine, and Belgravia, as well as in a number of short story book collections. These collections; The Seen and the Unseen (1900), Marvels and Mysteries (1900), Both Sides of the Veil (1901) and Between the Dark and the Daylight (1902) all feature an eclectic mix of humour, crime, romance and the occult.

He also published several serial short stories. Here he was able to develop characters whose adventures could be related in discrete stories across numerous editions of a magazine. An example is Mr. Pugh and Mr. Tress of Curios (1898). They are rival collectors between whom pass a series of bizarre and disturbing objects—poisoned rings, pipes which seem to come to life, a phonograph record on which a murdered woman seems to speak from the dead, and the severed hand of a 13th-century aristocrat.

During his career he sometimes came up with characters or stories ahead of their time. His character Miss Judith Lee, a young teacher of deaf pupils whose lip-reading ability involves her with mysteries that she solves by acting as a detective was very pro-active in this regard.

Richard Marsh died from heart disease in Haywards Heath in Sussex on 9th August 1915.

Several of his novels were published posthumously.

Richard Marsh – A Concise Bibliography

As Bernard Heldmann
Boxall School: A Tale of Schoolboy Life (1881)
Dorrincourt [Union Jack, April-September 1881]
Expelled: Being the Story of a Young Gentleman (1882)
Daintree (1883)

As Richard Marsh
Capturing a Convict (Strand Magazine 1893)
The Devil's Diamond (1893)
The Mahatma's Pupil (1893)
The Strange Wooing of Mary Bowler (1895)
Mrs Musgrave—and her Husband (1895)
The Mystery of Philip Bennion's Death (1897)

The Crime and the Criminal (1897)
The Duke and the Damsel (1897)
The Beetle: A Mystery (1897)
The House of Mystery (1898)
Under One Cover: Eleven Stories by S. Baring-Gould, Richard Marsh, Ernest G. Henham, Fergus Hume, Andrew Merry and A. St John Adcock (1898)
Curios: Some Strange Adventures of Two Bachelors (1898)
Tom Ossington's Ghost (1898)
The Datchet Diamonds (1898)
The Woman with One Hand and Mr Ely's Engagement (1899)
In Full Cry (1899)
Frivolities: Especially Addressed to Those Who Are Tired of Being Serious (1899)
The Purse Which Was Found
For One Night Only
Returning a Verdict
The Chancellor's Ward
A Honeymoon Trip
The Burglar's Blunder
Ninepence
A Battlefield Up-to-date
Mr. Harland's Pupils
A Burglar Alarm
A Lesson in Sculling
Outside
The Chase of the Ruby (1900)
An Aristocratic Detective (1900)
A Hero of Romance (1900)
The Seen and the Unseen (1900)
The Goddess: A Demon (1900)
Ada Vernham, Actress (1900)
A Second Coming (1900)
Marvels and Mysteries (1900)
The Long Arm of Coincidence
The Mask
An Experience
Pourquoipas
By Suggestion
A Silent Witness
To Be Used Against Him
The Words of a Little Child
How He Passed!
The Joss: A Reversion (1901)
Both Sides of the Veil (1901)
Amusement Only (1901)
The Twickenham Peerage (1902)
Between the Dark and the Daylight (1902)
The Adventures of Augustus Short: Things Which I Have Done for Others and Wish I Hadn't (1902)
A Metamorphosis (1903)

The Death Whistle (1903)
The Magnetic Girl (1903)
Miss Arnott's Marriage (1904)
Garnered (1904)
A Duel (1904)
A Spoiler of Men (1905)
The Marquis of Putney (1905)
The Confessions of a Young Lady (1905)
Under One Flag (1906)
In the Service of Love (1906)
The Garden of Mystery (1906)
A Woman Perfected (1907)
The Romance of a Maid of Honour (1907)
The Girl and the Miracle (1907)
The Surprising Husband (1908)
The Coward behind the Curtain (1908)
That Master of Ours (1908)
A Royal Indiscretion (1909)
The Interrupted Kiss (1909)
The Girl in the Blue Dress (1909)
The Lovely Mrs Blake (1910)
Live Men's Shoes (1910)
The Twin Sisters (1911)
A Drama of the Telephone (1911)
Violet Forster's Lover (1912)
Sam Briggs: His Book (1912)
Judith Lee: Some Pages from her Life (1912)
The Master of Deception (1913)
Justice—Suspended (1913)
If It Please You (1913)
The Woman in the Car (1914)
Molly's Husband (1914)
Margot—and her Judges (1914)
The Man with Nine Lives (1915)
Love in Fetters (1915)
His Love or his Life (1915)
The Flying Girl (1915)
Violet Forster's Lover (1916)
The Adventures of Judith Lee (1916)
Sam Briggs, V.C. (1916)
Coming of Age (1916)
The Great Temptation (1916)
The Deacon's Daughter (1917)
On the Jury (1918)
Orders to Marry ([1918)
Outwitted (1919)
Apron-Strings (1920)

Periodicals

For Debt, Windsor Magazine (January 1902)
Returning a Verdict, Cornhill Magazine (January 1896)
The Lost Duchess, Cornhill Magazine (January 1895)
Mrs Riddles Daughter, All the Year Round (17 March 1894)
An Episcopal Scandal, Cornhill Magazine (February 1894)
A Rubber or Two, All the Year Round (16 September 1893)
A First Night, Cornhill Magazine (April 1893)
The Mystery of Philip Bennion's Death, Household Words (3/10/17/24/31 December 1892)
The Princess Margaretta, Household Words (3 December 1892)
The Puzzle, Cornhill Magazine (November 1892)
A Victim to Art, All the Year Round (2 July 1892)
The Burglar's Blunder, Derby Mercury (24 June 1891)
Pourquoipas, All the Year Round (9/16 May 1891)
The Pipe, Cornhill Magazine (March 1891)
When Greek Joined Greek, Household Words (6 September 1890)
His First Experiment, Cornhill Magazine (September 1890)
"Mignonette", All the Year Round (9 August 1890)
The Long Arm of Coincidence, Household Words (24 May 1890)
The Match of the Season, Cornhill Magazine (May 1890)
A Set of Chessmen, Cornhill Magazine (April 1890)
A Dream of Diamonds, Household Words (7 December 1889)
My Uncle's Flirtation, Household Words (16 November 1889)
"Em", Household Words (2 November 1889)
The Barnes Mystery: An Adventure of Judith Lee, Strand Magazine (October 1916)
"Scandalous!", Strand Magazine (August 1916)
What Fell on her Hat, Strand Magazine (April 1916)
The Adventures of Sam Briggs: On the Film, Strand Magazine (March 1916)
A Set of Chessmen, Cassell's Magazine of Fiction and Popular Literature (Dec 1915)
Sam Briggs Becomes a Soldier: A Fighting Man, Strand Magazine (December 1915)
Sam Briggs Becomes a Soldier: On the Way Home, Strand Magazine (November 1915)
Sam Briggs Becomes a Soldier: An Official Mistake, Strand Magazine (October 1915)
Sam Briggs Becomes a Soldier: In their Own Gas, Strand Magazine (September 1915)
Sam Briggs Becomes a Soldier: Sanctuary, Strand Magazine (August 1915)
Sam Briggs Becomes a Soldier: In the Nick of Time, Strand Magazine (July 1915)
Sam Briggs Becomes a Soldier: A Night Surprise for the Germans, Strand Magazine (June 1915)
Sam Briggs Becomes a Soldier: In the Trenches, Strand Magazine (May 1915)
Sam Briggs Becomes a Soldier: Baptism of Fire, Strand Magazine (April 1915)
Sam Briggs Becomes a Soldier: Two Stripes, Strand Magazine (March 1915)
Life in the King's New Army: Jack Carpenter's True Story, VI: Career for our Boys, Daily Mail (27 February 1915)
Life in the King's New Army: Jack Carpenter's True Story, V: The Tailor and the Man, Daily Mail (26 February 1915)
Life in the King's New Army: Jack Carpenter's True Story, IV: Hutments', Daily Mail (25 February 1915)

Life in the King's New Army: Jack Carpenter's True Story, III: First-Rate Fighting Men', Daily Mail (24 February 1915)

Life in the King's New Army: Jack Carpenter's True Story, II: The Berwick Borderers, Daily Mail (23 February 1915)

Life in the King's New Army: Jack Carpenter's True Story, I: Crossed Swords, Daily Mail (22 February 1915)

Sam Briggs Becomes a Soldier: A Man in the Making, Strand Magazine (February 1915)

Sam Briggs Becomes a Soldier: Sam Briggs Becomes a Soldier, Strand Magazine (January 1915)

The Amazing Visitor, Strand Magazine (December 1914)

Looping the Loop: An Adventure of Sam Briggs, Strand Magazine (August 1914)

The Torch, Strand Magazine (October 1913)

"Gaiety" Abroad, Strand Magazine (September 1913), 274-82

A Self-Appointed Guardian, English Illustrated Magazine (August 1913)

For the Cause, Strand Magazine (April 1913)

The Adventures of Judith Lee: The Affair of the Montagu Diamonds, Strand Magazine (February 1913)

The Adventures of Judith Lee: Mandragora, Strand Magazine (August 1912)

The Adventures of Judith Lee: "8 Elm Grove—Back Entrance", Strand Magazine (July 1912)

The Adventures of Judith Lee: The Restaurant Napolitain, Strand Magazine (June 1912)

The Adventures of Judith Lee: Uncle Jack, Strand Magazine (May 1912)

The Adventures of Judith Lee: Was It by Chance Only? Strand Magazine (April 1912)

The Adventures of Judith Lee: Isolda, Strand Magazine (March 1912)

The Adventures of Judith Lee: "Auld Lang Syne", Strand Magazine (January 1912)

The Adventures of Judith Lee: The Miracle, Strand Magazine (December 1911)

The Adventures of Judith Lee: Matched

The Burglary in Berkeley Square, Pearson's Magazine (December 1908)

The River of Light, Strand Magazine (December 1908)

The Girl in the Light Blue Dress, Strand Magazine (October 1908)

O'Rourke of the Saucy Sixth, Grand Magazine (June 1908)

The Adventures of Sam Briggs: The Limerick, Strand Magazine (February 1908)

The Adventures of Sam Briggs: The Star of Romance, Strand Magazine (July 1907)

The Adventures of Sam Briggs: A Social Evening, Strand Magazine (April 1907)

My Best Story and Why I Think So No. 21: The Strange Occurrences in Canterstone Gaol, Grand Magazine (October 1906)

The Adventures of Sam Briggs: That Hansom, Strand Magazine (May 1906)

The Adventures of Sam Briggs: Her Fourth, Strand Magazine (December 1905)

The Adventures of Sam Briggs: A Modest Half-Crown, Strand Magazine (November 1905)

The Adventures of Sam Briggs: The Gift Horse, Strand Magazine (March 1905)

My Wedding Day, Strand Magazine (January 1905)

The Adventures of Sam Briggs: The Girl on the Sands, Strand Magazine (October 1904)

The Parson, the Soldier, and the Child, London Magazine (November 1903)

The Girl and the Boy, London Magazine (October 1903)

By Whose Hand? New Short Novel by Richard Marsh, Answers (1 August – 31 October 1903)

A Girl Who Couldn't, Strand Magazine (January 1903)

The Kit-Bag, Windsor Magazine, 17 (January 1903), 298-309

Their Reasons: Two Hitherto Unreported Conversations, House Annual (1902)

At Large: Being the Strange Perils and Experiences of George Otway, Suspect, Answers (12 July - 27 December 1902)

The Handwriting, Strand Magazine (June 1902)

La Haute Finance, Windsor Magazine (March 1902)

A Wonderful Girl, Strand Magazine (March 1902)

Skittles, English Illustrated Magazine, (February/March 1902)

Breaking the Ice, Strand Magazine (February 1902)

My Aunt's Excursion, Windsor Magazine (January 1902)

The Haunted Chair: The Story of a Strange Mystery, Harmsworth London Magazine (January 1902)

Miss Donne's Great Gamble, Strand Magazine (November 1901)

The Man in the Glass Cage; or The Strange Story of the Twickenham Peerage, Manchester Times, (6 September – 27 December 1901

The Adventures of Augustus Short: Things Which I Have Done for Others, and Wish I Hadn't: The Address Which I Gave for Rudman, Cassell's Magazine (November 1901)

The Adventures of Augustus Short: Things Which I Have Done for Others, and Wish I Hadn't: Jones's Love Affair, Cassell's Magazine (October 1901)

The Adventures of Augustus Short: Things Which I Have Done for Others, and Wish I Hadn't: The Duel I Fought of Jarvis, Cassell's Magazine (September 1901)

The Adventures of Augustus Short: Things Which I Have Done for Others, and Wish I Hadn't: Griffin's Offspring, Cassell's Magazine (August 1901)

The Adventures of Augustus Short: Things Which I Have Done for Others, and Wish I Hadn't: McCulloch's Shoes, Cassell's Magazine (July 1901)

The Adventures of Augustus Short: Things Which I Have Done for Others, and Wish I Hadn't: The Fitzroy-Jenkinsons' Rooms, Cassell's Magazine (June 1901)

Staggers, Windsor Magazine (April 1901)

How I Drove a Motor Car for Randal, Strand Magazine (April 1901)

The Disappearance of Mrs Macrecham: The Amazing Story of a Strange Cat, Harmsworth Monthly Pictorial Magazine (March 1901)

The Irregularity of the Juryman, Strand Magazine (December 1900)

The Strange Fortune of Pollie Blythe: The Story of a Chinese "God", Manchester Times (12 October 1900 – 8 February 1901)

Pugh's Poisoned Ring, Harmsworth Monthly Pictorial Magazine (October 1900)

Willyum, Penny Illustrated Paper and Illustrated Times, (26 May 1900)

Willyum, Hampshire Telegraph and Naval Chronicle (26 May 1900)

The Goddess: A Demon, Manchester Times (12 January – 30 March 1900)

The Stolen Treaty, Manchester Times (27 October 1899)

For One Night Only, Answers (8 April 1899)

In Full Cry, Manchester Times (3 March – 9 June 1899)

The Colonel's Cane, Cassell's Magazine (February 1899)

The Burglary at Azalea Villa, Manchester Times, (13 January 1899)

The Burglary at Azalea Villa, Newcastle Weekly Courant (14 January 1899)

Our Christmas Burglar, Answers (17 December 1898)

Something to his Advantage, Manchester Times (7 October – 4 November 1898)

A Lesson in Sculling, Newcastle Weekly Courant (October 1898)

That Five Hundred Pound Price, Harmsworth Monthly Pictorial Magazine (September 1898)

The Chancellor's Ward, Harmsworth Monthly Pictorial Magazine (August 1898)

The Ossington Mystery, Ipswich Journal (1 April – 17 June 1898)

The Duchess of Datchet's Diamonds, New Zealand Graphic and Ladies' Journal (New Zealand) (7 May – 25 June 1898)

The Peril of Paul Lessingham: The Story of a Haunted Man, Answers (13 March – 19 June 1897)

The Purse Which Was Found, Answers (17 April 1897)

The Rector and the Curate, Answers (19 December 1896)
An Illustration of Modern Science, Pall Mall Magazine (November 1896)
A Battlefield Up-to-Date, Idler Magazine (August 1896)
Twins, Idler Magazine (January 1896)
Lady Wishaw's Hand, Leeds Mercury (January 1895)
Young George, St Nicholas (March 1894)
Exchange Is Robbery, Idler Magazine (December 1893 - January 1894)
The Tipster: An Impossible Story, Home Chimes (December 1893)
The Influence of Women, Home Chimes (November 1893)
By Deputy: A Reminiscence of Travel, Home Chimes (October 1893)
Rivals, Home Chimes (September 1893)
Capturing a Convict, Strand Magazine (August 1893)
A Burglar Alarm, Home Chimes (June 1893)
Music Halls and Theatres, Home Chimes (March 1893)
A Strange Bride, Manchester Times (6/13 January 1893)
The Mask, Gentleman's Magazine (December 1892)
A Vision of the Night, Strand Magazine (December 1892)
Nelly, Home Chimes (November 1892)
A Prophet: A Story, New England Magazine (October - November 1892)
Mr Harland's Pupils, Home Chimes (August 1892)
The Brothers in Grey, Home Chimes (April 1892)
The Half-Back, Derby Mercury (March 1892)
The Half-Back, Home Chimes (February 1892)
The Violin, Home Chimes (December 1891)
The Short Story, Home Chimes (August 1891)
Magical Music, Gentleman's Magazine (May 1891)
A Honeymoon Trip, Home Chimes (April 1891)
Mitwaterstraand, Time (September 1890)
A Pack of Cards, Longman's Magazine (August 1890)
The Burglar's Blunder, Ladies' Journal (Canada) (1 July 1890)
The Strange Occurrences in Canterstone Jail, Blackwood's Edinburgh Magazine (June 1890)
A Substitute: The Story of My Last Cricket-Match, Longman's Magazine (June 1890)
The Burglar's Blunder, Gentleman's Magazine (May 1890)
A Silent Witness, Belgravia (October 1889)
A Bed for the Night, Belgravia (Summer 1889)
Payment for a Life, Belgravia (Summer 1888)